The Current of Water

J. A. Zilske

Books by J. A. Zilske

Fiction:
The Invitation
The Invitation: The Play

Nonfiction:
The Hope Shift
Words of Worship
Elements of Life
A Season of Giving
A Season of Giving for Children

Children's Fiction and Activity Books:
The Saurus
Dreaming in Color
Dreaming in Color—Interactive Drawing and Writing Book
Jackson McDoo and Donny, Too
Jackson McDoo and Donny, Too—Parent/Teacher Guide
The Best Christmas Ever

Poetry:
Licking the Dust: Poems from the Little Ease

Cover Art: J. A. Zilske

1st edition 2023

Praise for *The Current of Water*

"*The Current of Water* by J. A. Zilske will sweep you away. The stories of the women this novel follows are haunting, painful, and beautiful. Zilske writes with a voice that draws you in and you immediately make a heart-connection to the characters. *The Current of Water* is a bittersweet tale of loves, losses, and triumphs written with almost hypnotic prose."

Heather Blaton USA Today Best-Selling Author

"Brilliantly written, *The Current of Water* takes the reader through the ebb and flow of life storms and gentle streams sharing lessons learned through the centuries and seasons of a family and a country torn by racism, war, depression, addiction, and abuse. J. A. Zilske is a powerful writer who draws us in to the joys and trials every family relates to and the realization that 'God is always at work, and trust me, He's not done yet.'"

Elaine W. Miller, Author of *We All Married Idiots: Three Things You Will Never Change About Your Marriage and Ten Things You Can* and *Praise the Lord and Pass the Chemo: A Hopeful Response to a Hard Reality*

"*The Current of Water* is an exquisitely written, riveting, multi-generational page-turner that I couldn't put down. J.A. Zilske uses words the way an artist uses paint to bring stories to visual life. Through the powerful narratives of this genealogy of women, we experience their anguish and their hopes. We see the impact decisions and emotions have upon those who are scarred and those who are redeemed, and are moved to examine our own actions and conscience. And we glimpse the life-changing power of a gentle, loving Savior who brings peace and reconciliation."

Susan Allen Panzica, Author, Speaker, Anti-trafficking Advocate; book titles: *Mary had a little Lamb*, *The Quest*

"Raw, honest, unapologetic and redemptive are the words that spring to mind after reading J.A. Zilske's *The Current of Water*. The reality that life experiences can leave wounds that are raw and festering is made very evident in the lives of the women of this book. The author's presentation of characters honest and unapologetic in how they feel about their tragedies and how it has caused them to question their faith is refreshing. My heart was drawn to these women, and like their grandmother, Iris, I too was waiting and hoping for them to find true redemption from the only One who could fully heal and restore them. J.A. Zilske's style in writing has always been one to foster hope and this latest book will not disappoint. It causes us to look at ourselves in these women and be honest. Do we too question God and His ways? Have we also lost our faith, needing His Spirit to be the current pulling us into deeper waters with Him? I highly recommend you to walk through the pages of *The Current of Water*, sharing decades of pain and soul searching, to be filled with redemptive hope in the end. You will be blessed you came along with these ladies."

Laurie Ferris, author of *Thabo's Village, Soul Piercing, Consider His Heart, Lessons Along the Way, Even More Precious.*

"It's amazing to see how the stories of tragedy, grief and pain in *The Current of Water* are passed on through generations, and yet they manifest differently in those who receive them. They can become a legacy of grief, shame, and self-loathing, themes which can ruin lives, or become an inheritance of beautiful redemption which leads to healing and forgiveness. This is very familiar in its grief but also in its hope and healing for those of us who have found the Savior of our lives. I believe this story, rich in His grace and redemption, becomes very personal for a lot of us. An excellent read."

Nancy Lightbody, Women's Ministry and Retreat Coordinator

"J. A. Zilske's new release, *The Current of Water*, is a refreshing tale of how one woman's life leaves a legacy. As you relate, you see the impact of one mother's decision, and how over the years and generations, healing and hope are possible."

Lisa Buske, author, *One Sister's Journey*, Keeping it Real Podcast ~ Blog ~ Inspirational Speaker

Contents

Dedication

To all who are searching

and to all who have been found.

And to the One who has swept me away.

I give these words back to You

for Your glory.

Acknowledgments

I want to thank Evelyn J. Wagoner for her incredible editing talents. Because of her eye for detail and ability to ask probing questions, she made revising something I looked forward to. Really.

Thank you to Pam and Matt for your continued editorial support and your brilliant suggestions. You were my much needed mini writing group.

Martha, my creative partner, you never let me slack off. Thank you for keeping me on track, even when I was ready to give up.

Cheri, you are precious to me for your unwavering belief that this was a story worthy to be told.

To all who allowed me to brainstorm when I was at an impasse, who read and reread my many drafts, I thank you all for your continued patience and encouragement.

Laurie, I thank you for your proofreading help. You expertly found what I missed and helped me through those final steps.

I am so very grateful to all my dear sisters—to my Nancy and all my Jersey Girls who daily cover me with prayer and inspire me along the way. I am blessed beyond measure.

A Family of Women

Iris: 1800-1889

Elizabeth: 1857-1943

Flora: 1868-1942

Merriam: 1878-1915

Mary Rose: 1895-1928

Mabel: 1904-1979

Edith: 1923-1987

Helen: 1928-1992

Esther: 1940-

Minerva: 1943-

Mary Agnes: 1947-

Genevieve/Eve: 1949-

Alice: 1952-2019

Harriet: 1963-

Carlotta: 1972-

Esther Ruth: 1980-

The Current of Water

I am drawn to You, called like a wave
toward the shore.
My conscience, held
in the rebel thrill
of an unauthorized fire, tries to close
the gap between yes and no—futile
without a horizon. The rituals
of dead patriarchs, who have excluded
my feminine heart, fail me. I am

passionately abandoned, set adrift
by a dynamic breeze-sigh that speaks to
the hidden depth of my need. The pull

.

is strong. One foot poised above
the turbulent flow, that moment
between breaths when a word
slices open the current of possibility.

I am
swept away.

Alice, 2017

Prologue

Iris

1800-1889

The day after I turned fifteen I married. My father, weakened from the fever that took my mother, made an arrangement with a man named Walter, someone he believed to be honorable. Even though I had only met him once, I accepted without question being taught that obedience was more important than affection.

After my father died, we came to these northern lands of New York to flee what my husband called the disease and sinful squalor of the cities—another hasty decision made without my consent.

Unrest and fear daily circled our small homestead and threatened to divide us. As I leaned ever deeper on the scriptures promising eternal safety, my husband became doubtful, unsettled in his manner. This disquiet increased when our daughter, Abigail, was born. His need to protect grew around us like the stones he piled around our land.

October 1819

It was one of those sweet October days, leaves just beginning to fall like a gentle spring shower. A slight breeze cooled the sweat from my collar, the sun still warm on my face. Churning always did cause me to perspire.

My hands, calloused from the work of creating a life in this wilderness, firm around the wooden dasher, pulsed out a rhythm that repeated with every push and pull.

I realized I was humming a bit too loud when I glanced over at Abigail, our first surviving daughter. Even at her young age, I noticed a slight look of judgment instead of amusement. I wondered if she would ever understand the pleasure I felt as my spirit blended with His Spirit even in this seemingly endless toil—the need for prayer for her, for her daughters.

I cry to the One who hears me.

With every plunge of the wood into milk becoming more I found myself repeating the words—*satisfy their thirst and guide them with the unseen hands of Your love.*

A Necessary Melting

Merriam

1878-1915

I watch the tallow drip sideways, down the tapered cone, a necessary melting surrounded by a haze, giving erratic light to my weary evenings. We sit, silent once the children are asleep, wrapped in the stilted glow.

I married Charles in 1895 when I was seventeen. He called me beautiful, but I knew the truth—it was my feigned inhibitions he thought the secret to my beauty.

My father, strict and somewhat unfeeling I thought, tried his best to instill his staid legacy deep within me. Mother's faith kept her intact but unable to push against her husband's edicts. This conflicting affected each of us children differently. My brothers took to dominating any and everything they could; my sisters, quiet and obedient, thrived only in each other's company. For me, the youngest, a passionate dissatisfaction hid beneath my compliance. For as long as I could remember, I had a fervent need to take wild chances, want untamed adventure. When the time came, my father firmly believed a man like Charles would "settle" me.

Two years before we married, Charles had taken over his family's business, a mercantile, a worthy calling providing necessities. His parents died shortly before his eighteenth birthday, leaving him, the eldest, to become the man his grandfather often doubted he'd ever become. His father went out railing against an unknown, angry the world had withheld its bounty. His mother followed two days later, a quiet accepting, a sturdy confidence in what lay beyond.

One night when Charles lay deep in a fever, he told me about his mother as he swatted at his delusions. A woman, he said, he never understood but thought he loved. Her fervent prayers spoken over him at night, words of hope and a future, words he now thought just as delusional as his feverish shadows.

The children came quickly, the only release for both of us. Mary Rose was the first—a disappointment we shared, although not for the same reasons. Charles' grandfather just scowled over the sex of his first great-grandchild, breeding a discontentment in my husband that followed him for years. I, on the other hand, felt disappointment in Mary's apparent contentment—content at my breast, content in the cradle, content with whatever was given or withheld. There was a part of me that wanted her to scream her need, not accept, not settle.

Our dear James was born eleven months later, but his weak cries were heard for only two days before his tiny form disappeared from our lives. Emma, conceived in our grief, thrived from her first bold cry, a sound that would seal the closeness we shared until she passed from my sight seven months later, taken by the same sickness that claimed her namesake, Charles' beloved grandmother.

My husband turned to his mother's faith, every night repeating the scriptures promising everlasting life and peace that was beyond understanding. The words comforted him but only skimmed the surface of the deep loss I felt, a hollow hurt that words could not fill.

Two years passed before our son, David, was born. Strong and healthy, he became a confirmative stamp on Charles' waning manhood. David thrived those first years, adventuresome beyond his ability to discern danger. He had an intense need even at that age to follow his father, showing worth.

The well had been an addition last year, us being a distance from the stream, meant to quench thirst and preserve precious milk and butter. David would watch his father and me as we'd lower the buckets down the cool shaft to place or retrieve. We thought the words of caution we spoke enough, but children see adventure too easy and danger too late. He disappeared before any of us could see his fault.

I believed myself to be alone responsible for David's death. I should have had an innate sense of his wanderings, followed every step, known every rung. Even though I knew dear Mary Rose held some of the blame on her young shoulders, I was unable to absolve her from this guilt which imbedded its culpable narrative deep within our flawed feminine hearts.

Charles became almost driven, becoming the man whose qualities other women desired to see in their husbands. He poured his grief into birthing a successful business, something he could control. In response to my withdrawing, he doted on Mary, even though in his eyes one girl still did not add up to one boy.

Since that heartrending day, I held life in a tight embrace, desperate to warn, to avert every curious step. Because of this, Mary was, at times, sullen and remote, drawing away from me, clinging instead to her father. I never shared with her the youthful stories of my imagined adventures, ones buried beneath responsibility that ultimately left us all wanting more.

A quiet would fall over our household each evening like the mist that hung over the small pond, stifling the crickets and frogs into a dull background, a collective exhale into the wavering shadows.

I secretly wanted to be like my great-grandmother, Iris, whose feet would tap to her joyful humming while she churned or spun. My grandmother told me when she was young she was embarrassed by the sounds, frivolous noises she called them, distracting from the severity of a woman's lot—a lot she passed on to my mother and to me.

1915

I hear a woman's voice humming to her Savior as I lay here, held in the grip of a fever brought on by Andrew's birth, the son of my despair. I am fading beneath the heat—a necessary melting surrounded by a haze.

Mary Rose

1895-1928

Death and disease were common callers in the days surrounding the dawn of a new century. Uncertainty loomed with every birth, with every life a hesitant living. I watched many around me claim to trust a greater good in loss. Unsure of how to find deep and lasting comfort in a God I was only casually acquainted with, my life circled around belief, making me doubt the wisdom of their faith.

Ever since I could remember there had been this rift within me. Named for a woman held in high esteem, I swung like a pendulum between beloved and bitter, monogrammed by a fate I didn't understand.

I was too young to remember James who passed from our lives, a brief shadow, known to me only as a wooden cross near the garden. When I was about three, Emma was born. I thought her a doll at first, something to distract, to amuse. She was a child who made herself known, whether demanding the breast or craving attentive arms her infectious disposition charmed us all.

It wasn't until three days after she died that I began to understand how death could define and shroud. I had been sent to a neighbor when the sickness first appeared thinking in my young mind I was somehow being punished for tipping over the milk crock that morning. Four days later my father came to bring me home. His eyes, hollow with grief, stared past me as he took my hand in his. I told him I was sorry for the milk. He grasped my hand tighter and offered no other words except, "Mary, Emma has died." We walked back home in silence, the only sound the crunching of dried leaves, dead beneath our feet. I started to weep but the tightening of my father's grip told me to stop. It was then I learned to hold my tears like my mother did.

A few years later, David was born. My father behaved as if this was his first child, so proud, with an almost arrogant air of accomplishment. He beamed at every milestone—every step taken. It was as if each hesitant word David spoke came directly from the mouth of *his* worth.

In the beginning, I was cautious with my affection toward David. Somewhere in my young mind I carried a sense that if I had been different, better, Emma would not have died. Maybe it was just my gleaning off my mother's guilt. Maybe it was the depth of my father's love for his only son. Maybe it was just a forewarning of things to come.

I will never forget the day I never want to remember. There was a slight chill in the air. The sky, blue beyond blue, met the fiery colors that still clung to the branches above us. The leaves were crisp beneath our feet as we played. The sound, familiar yet overlooked by my young mind, made David laugh. He was always running, arms waving, his little voice shouting.

Hide and seek was David's favorite game. He loved to squat down beside the wood pile or stand so still behind a too small tree and me pretending not to see his little arms hugging its narrow base. Mother had told me to watch him while she hung the wash, nothing unusual.

As I hid my eyes and counted to ten, I thought I heard a small cry, but I brushed it aside as just a sign of David's excitement.

"Ten! Here I come, David. I'll find you today!" I looked behind the wood pile and around the trees that circled our home. "Hmm. I wonder where David is?" saying loud enough for him to hear. "He must be hiding someplace new."

After checking all his usual places I finally said, "You win, David. Come out now."

Silence.

I turned at the slight sound of leaves falling to the ground behind me. I began to shout his name. "David!" This brought my mother around the house.

"What's all this shouting for?"

The look on my face said it all. We began to call him, our eyes searching the surrounding field. We both saw it at the same time—a board had been slid away. We ran down the small hill toward the well. I knew before I got there David was dead, dead because I had not been vigilant. The well, meant to make our lives easier, had become a grave.

The days palpitated between a blur and a vivid nightmare. All I knew was that, once again, I was alone.

In the weeks and months that followed, every time I walked past the now abandoned well I felt sick and guilty, something my mother and I equally shared.

Ever since my brother died last year, Sunday afternoons were reserved for visiting Elizabeth, my father's spinster sister, who chose to live out her life away from a world she was ill-fitted for. Her home was a small cabin built by her fiancé, long gone but alive within the timbers. It was a modest build, nestled among the pines that framed the lake, almost picturesque with its rough hewn walls and simple necessities. Elizabeth was at peace with her lot, something we all desperately needed to understand.

Our visits became less frequent as the years passed, but the year I turned thirteen my father made it a point to resume our weekly trips. When I questioned him, he said, "It is for you to obey, Mary." Seeing my displeasure, he added, "It is best to remember what was before we accept what will be."

My parents were fearful of how quickly the world was changing, a vanishing of tradition and faith they said. I was curious but my parents were apprehensive. My father's response was to hold me and my mother close afraid we too would vanish—a familial suffocation he thought necessary.

My aunt fascinated me. I admired her independence from the convention that even now sought to mold and press me. Until she purchased an automobile, she would walk a mile five days a week to teach at the small school in town. When I asked if she minded doing all that walking she just smiled, patted my hand and said I'd understand her "steps of prayer" when I got older. I didn't believe then I'd ever get old enough to understand.

As the years passed, I looked forward to Sundays with Aunt Elizabeth and appreciated the peculiar peace that fell on us all when we were there. One weekend while we sipped our tea, I asked why she loved living so far from others.

My aunt looked at me and said, "Mary, let's take a walk down by the water, just you and me."

I was surprised she wanted to leave the warmth of the cabin and venture out into the cold. It had been flurrying, promising snowfall by day's end.

"Not too long you two. We need to be going soon before it gets dark."

"We won't be long, Papa" We bundled up and headed down the dirt path to the lake. A brisk wind came up and made Elizabeth squeal with delight. She pulled her hat back down over her graying hair. "Come on. We better hurry or we'll blow away before we can get to the end of the trail."

I put my head down against the wind and walked ahead. When I got to the bend, I noticed my aunt had stopped behind me.

I walked back and said, "Is something wrong? Are you tired?"

She put her gloved hands on my shoulders and held me firm. "Mary Rose, what do you see when you look at your feet?"

I was startled because my full name was rarely spoken and only used on serious occasions. "My feet?" I looked down at the rough path. Quietly I said, "I look down…so I won't trip."

She lifted my chin and looked intently into my eyes. Gesturing to the surrounding scene she said, "Now what do you see?"

I stood almost breathless. I realized from her serious tone there was something more she wanted me to understand. I blinked back the cold and not knowing what else to say said, "Well, I see trees, lots of trees." When my aunt didn't respond I added, "And there, I can see a small part of the lake." I pointed. "You see? There down the path." Elizabeth smiled and nodded her approval.

Walking arm in arm toward the water's edge she said, "Tell me more."

I sensed an impatience rising up in me but managed a weak smile nonetheless. I turned this way and that, taking in everything around me. "I like the way the pine's prickly needles stay green all year. They don't die out when the cold comes. But some of those trees over there have lost their leaves and look somewhat sad to me. That branch there, see it? It looks like a really old person's finger, all craggy and bent."

She laughed at the image. "That's very good. Now what do you hear?"

I closed my eyes and listened as the wind came and went in waves, pulsing like an uneven heartbeat.

"Oh, Aunt Elizabeth, the wind almost sounds like its breathing, coming and going like that. I know it's foolish…"

"Mary, there's nothing foolish about looking deeper into what God has laid before us. What can you smell?"

I took a deep breath of the cold air and said, "Pine—ah, reminds me of Christmas. There's also the smoke from your cabin. I like that smell."

"As do I." She closed her eyes and took in a slow breath. A lone tear ran down her cheek.

"Oh, Auntie, are you alright?"

"I'm fine, dear."

"But why are you crying?"

"Oh, I always get emotional when I'm surrounded by what I love." She tightened her scarf and looked up at the disappearing sun. "I suppose we ought to get back or they'll be wondering what happened to us."

"But what about the lake?"

She smiled and put her arm around me. "Another day, dear one. There's always another day."

As we came around the bend and saw the cabin, she stopped. "Mary, I hope one day you and your daughters will come here if it's still standing." My aunt turned to me and with a serious tone said, "Never forget how to listen to the wind, breathe in the scents of God's design and see what He has done around you." She cupped my face with both of her hands. "Always keep your eyes fixed on Jesus and on the wonder of what lies ahead. Leave the details of the path to God."

"I'll never forget, Auntie. I promise." But I did forget. It would be years before I allowed her words to return and accuse.

Months turned into years, a hollow progress that dulled all our senses. My life was predictable to a fault, at least until the day I stepped out from the measured current that had defined me and stepped blindly into the deep of a violent flow.

I had never seen such a symbiotic agreement between earth and sky as I did that day when I first met Edward. Leaves on the verge—a last hurrah before dying—voracious in their need for color. Red, yellow, orange all competing for attention. The sky, as if offering the only missing tone, was a sapphire backdrop beyond my reach. I shivered at the sight but brushed off the feeling of forewarning. For a moment my eyes were drawn upward, away from what lay in front of me. I should have heeded the significance of its meaning, but I shook it off as one does a chill.

I had wandered down by the lake, a brief respite from my parents' watchful eyes. That's when I saw him pulling in a small boat, dragging it through the rough sand, his hair tossed across a sweaty forehead. He glanced over toward me and brazenly smiled. I shrank into the tree line but as I looked back, I could see him smirk. It made my heart shiver.

I thought I was in love as do all foolish females. I was at the age when most around me had already begun to marry. I stayed with my parents believing if I left them they would both sink down and drown, just like David.

There were those in town who thought Edward to be a somewhat brash young man who believed the world would bow to his needs. I didn't understand their judgments then. All I could see was his bold manner, something I regrettably mistook for confidence.

When I was younger, I had heard stories, spoken low and discreet about the errant son who left to make his way up north. Once when my father and I saw his mother in town she told us her son was visiting to restock his resources. My father glanced at the scowling man whose loud voice could be heard arguing with the storekeeper and said, “How nice for you.”

“Yes. I must be leaving.” It was all she said as she excused herself and hurriedly walked toward her son. On our way home my father warned, said a fear circled her smile.

But being young and naïve, I didn’t regard the warning. Edward returned home three times over the next few years, each time he sought me out, whittled down my reserve. He was twenty-five when we ran away to wed against my father’s wishes. The year was 1914, and I was nineteen.

It was one week after we moved to the small cabin that he first struck me. It came like a swift rage across my face. He had been drinking and said I was moving too slow getting his dinner. I was too stunned to do anything, but I moved faster.

The next year I gave birth to a son which eased Edward’s hostility toward me. At least until the child began to weaken. My dear boy died three weeks later, slipping away without a sound. Edward blamed me, said I wasn’t woman enough to keep a male child alive. He repeated his hurtful and cruel remarks as we stood before Walter’s small grave. This began the unraveling of my already fragile sense of worth. If it was possible, I lost more than a child that day.

Edward spent more and more time away, coming home only to replenish his need and renew his disgust. I was never sure where he went or what he did. Once when I summoned up the courage to ask, he said all I needed to know was that he was a man who knew how to get what he wanted, how to win the respect of others. When he picked up his pack and headed for the door, he turned and faced me, making me step back fearing what came next, but all he said was, “You should be grateful I provide for you at all. Stop questioning me!” The force of the door's slam felt like a slap. I didn't realize I had been holding my breath until I began to feel unsteady.

When he was gone, I thrived. My garden, proof I could give life, sustained me. I fished in the stream and gleaned the rich berries that grew near a small abandoned cabin, lost back in the woods. The sight of the rough wood, the dismantled stone fireplace, and the smell of pine pulled at a memory left behind. Now a broken shell was all I had left.

I realized I was with child again but didn't tell Edward right away. I think I wanted to hold life to myself, for myself, as long as I could. When I did tell him, he said he hoped this time I would produce something of value. But, in his eyes, it was not to be.

Lillian was born into a divided world—her father's perpetual disappointment on one side and my furtive longing on the other. Even though she carried Edward's mother's name, a shell of a woman, her little life became my purpose, my salvation. Deep down I knew it was wrong to claim saving from any other than God but when one has so little the grasping comes to whatever is near.

Whenever I could get away, I would carry my girl to my hidden refuge away from the disapproving eyes of her father where I would speak soft imaginings of gracious neighbors and hospitable friends who would welcome us in. I told Lily about Aunt Elizabeth, speaking of remembered sights, leaving out the promises made and broken. It was a place of calm for me, a place where I could pretend all was as it should be. It was also where I first began to sense a forgotten presence and recall the distant musings of a vague faith.

After a particularly difficult afternoon, I picked up my daughter and told Edward I was going to go gather berries for a pie. He just responded with, "Might be gone by the time you get back." I just nodded, learned not to question.

My pace quickened as I turned the bend and saw my solitary sanctuary. I stopped and took a deep breath of the scented air. "We're here, my girl." I looked down and noticed she had fallen asleep in my arms. "That's good. Rest now. I think I'll do the same." As I pressed myself close against the cool stones, I closed my eyes. The spotty sunlight warmed my face. I began to rock my daughter and softly sing one of the hymns I used to love when I was young…

> "*Alone with Him, I find sweet rest. From all my troubles, on His breast; I cast on Him my every care, and find sweet peace and comfort there.*"

I laughed, marveling I remembered the words. Just then like a flash I saw the face of an old acquaintance of my father. Startled, I became uneasy at the force with which this uninvited vision intruded.

Lily began to whimper so, seeing there was no one around, I offered my breast which soothed her. I leaned back and allowed my thoughts to wander. Old Mrs. Clemmens. In my mind's eye, I could see her form, respectful and still. Her back straight as her age would allow—the very picture of piety.

Church was a rigid affair except for Mrs. Clemmens, a woman, widowed and alone, who would sit silent throughout the hours-long services, upright on a stiff bench. From the back she appeared as pious as the next but from the side one could see this simple smile that graced her wrinkled face. I never understood why, but now it was all that came to my mind—nothing about her tragic losses, her inadequate living conditions, or her noticeable limp. Nothing but that smile. I wondered if my lips would ever curl up into an otherworldly smile or would my sorrow-worn face never display anything but a countenance of regret.

One day about seven months after she was born, Lily's cry changed from one of need to one of pain. That morning I had left her alone with her father, something I rarely did, to deliver bread to an ailing neighbor. When I returned, Edward was pacing by the door.

"Where were you?" he demanded.

"Is everything all right?" I cautiously slipped past him, removing my coat.

"Nothing's all right! She won't stop crying."

His refusal to look at me warned, but I knew I needed to try and soothe, not accuse. I laid a hesitant hand on his back. "Edward."

He turned to me then, turned on me, swatting at my hand, raising his fist. Surprised at the firmness of my stance, he tightened his fingers. He glared at me but lowered his hand. He looked around like he had suddenly forgotten where he was. Edward stormed past me, motioning in the air.

"All of this…is your fault. *Your* fault!"

He roughly pushed past me and grabbed his coat. Lily's renewed cries stopped him mid stride. As he left, he tried to say something but just shook his head.

I started to go after him. "Edward! Where are you going?" As I watched him quickly disappear around the bend, I looked up at the darkening sky. Rain would come soon. As the cold wind picked up, I closed the door and hurried over to calm. When I picked Lily up, she cried even harder.

"Baby girl, what's the matter?" I laid her on the bed thinking she needed to be changed. It was then I noticed bruises around both of her small arms, imprints of Edward's rage. I started to cry. "What did he do to you?"

My anger seethed beneath the surface of my fear. I tried to calm her at my breast, but she refused. I looked into her cloudy eyes. Could she even see me? I exhaled the word "Enough" and gently wrapped her up. When I opened the door, a sharp light and thunderous clap jolted, and the heavens opened up their rage. Rain pounded down as the wind whipped at my face. I only got to the wood pile when I knew I needed to turn back.

Back inside, I stood numb before the waning fire. The only words that came were, "You won."

The next hours I tenderly held my daughter close as I railed against any and everything sacred. My words shouted as if in response to the shattering thunder. I called down curses on Edward and made promises to God that we both knew I couldn't keep. As the strength of my cries intensified, Lily's became less and less. Her breathing, shallow and weak, finally ended in a small but desperate gasp.

I sat and rocked her until the sun came up. The storm outside had passed, but the thunderous ache within me still pounded. As my heart beat against her lifeless form, I prayed it would cease so my pain would end like Lily's.

Later that day I wrapped my dead daughter in the small quilt I had made her and started walking, moving as one who lacked direction. I don't know how long I stood before his door trembling with the cold and the need for absolution.

"Mary?"

I heard his voice as if in a dream. Turning my head ever so slightly toward the sound I saw old Pastor Moore standing next to me with an armload of kindling.

"Mary, what's wrong?" He glanced at the bundle in my arms and said, "Is Lillian alright?"

My silence told him she was not. He hastily dropped the wood and tried to gently guide me.

"Come inside, dear."

I allowed him to lead, knowing I had no will of my own left.

"That's right. Come near the stove. It will take the chill off."

I stood in the parlor, grave still. He came close and tenderly pulled the small blanket away from the baby's still face.

"Oh, Mary, I'm so sorry. Here, let me take her."

I jerked his hand away. "No! I have to hold her, protect her."

"Lucile? Lucile! Come in here, please."

His wife hurried in and one look at us both told her everything—but not everything.

I laid my daughter to rest beside her brother, a strange comfort. Neighbors asked no questions about her passing, impolite to intrude, impossible to explain.

Apprehension and sorrow were a constant. My only refuge the deserted and broken dwelling where I once sang to my daughter and almost began to open my heart. Now it was just a bitter reminder that everything perished. Still, I found myself returning again and again, whether to restore or punish I could not tell.

Edward returned about two weeks later, claiming he had nothing to do with Lily's death. He said she rolled off the bed when he was changing her, that he never knew she was hurt. I was numb, barely hearing his words. Looking back, I'll never completely understand why I finally accepted his weak explanations. Perhaps it was because I was no longer capable of telling the difference between a lie and a truth—perhaps I just didn't care anymore.

Because life had a way of coming when it wills, I gave birth to another daughter in 1921, my only attendant being an impatient and disappointed husband. I asked Edward what he would like to name the child. I was hopeful as he leaned in and took the tiny form from my arms. As she began to cry, he roughly handed her back to me and said, "Doesn't matter."

I named her Mildred after a cherished childhood friend, a name that carried a gentle strength in its meaning. Millie learned to be quiet and content, something that saved her from the start. Two months after she was born Edward came home and told me to take the child and get out, that he had at last found a woman who could give him a son.

I gathered up what meager belongings I possessed and took Mildred to my father's house. It was a complicated release. I was angry not just at Edward but at the apparent smallness of my resolve. *I* should have left. *I* should have protected. *I* should have....Regrets, a constant companion on my journey home, badgered me, replaced that still, small voice with one of accusation, words that formed around me like a second skin.

My father welcomed me and my daughter, sorrowful he had not acted on his fears that I had made a terrible mistake. My father still grieved my mother, taken the previous year, leaving him with a bewildered two year old. His unmarried sister, Julia, came to live with him when my mother died but little Andrew's contrary disposition just bred discord. She was relieved when I came, not for familial reasons but for release from her duty.

As the years passed, things remained strained as Andrew was often cruel to Millie, something I could not abide. My father responded to his son's outbursts with his own, driving a wedge between us. This abrasiveness caused an added friction to an already heated atmosphere. The fire I had allowed to smolder around my daughter and me still followed and burned.

Millie and I settled into a cautious rhythm. My frequent, "We are guests here" taught her to be compliant whenever possible. I know I should have encouraged her to stand up to her young uncle's cruelty but his outbursts intimidated me, even at his young age.

In an attempt to appease my father while creating distance between Andrew and Millie, I offered to help him at the store. A few times a week I would gather up my daughter and head out to the mercantile. She loved the sights and smells of the store, taking pleasure in the attention of friendly customers. Andrew stayed home, attended by a neighbor who, strangely enough, only had good things to say about him.

I reconciled myself to living without companionship but when I was twenty-eight, I met Jonathan. He appeared to be a kind man, with deep green eyes and a welcoming personality. After discreetly listening in on his conversation with my father, I learned he lived a few miles down the road. He was unmarried, raised horses, and cared for an assortment of abused and injured animals, an interest passed down to him by his father. He also shared his space with his younger step-brother, William. I later discovered William had been injured as a child and was affected with a limp. Jonathan's generosity to his brother was a thoughtfulness that drew me to him.

Even though I had no idea if I was still married to Edward, never having received a notice of any kind, I watched him closely. I could see Jonathan was everything Edward was not, but for a strange sense of propriety, I resisted his attention. I told him I would never marry again had I the opportunity, that his efforts would be best spent on someone else. He didn't push, just respectfully made his intentions known if and when I was ready.

One afternoon he asked if I would like to come to his farm, said his mare had birthed a healthy foal.

"Ah, Mary, you should see her. She's strong but gentle. She's a beauty. Named her Courage. I know. A strange name for a horse but fits her. Even though the birth was difficult, she came into the world wanting to live. Stood up shaky after a few tries 'bout thirty minutes later. Nursed right away too."

When I hesitated he said, "Of course, Millie should come. She's young but never too early to see new life already standing on its own."

Jonathan was right. Not only was Courage beautiful, she was full of life. I stood close, wanting to breathe in her vigor, her bold spirit. When I looked over to Jonathan, he was smiling and talking softly to my daughter. He had taken her in his arms to allow her to see and safely touch. It was then I knew Millie and I would always be protected, always be loved.

As the year 1922 came to a close, I read in the newspaper Edward had been shot and left for dead near the same abandoned shack where I had once found refuge. A sad regret briefly surfaced, but the release his death brought me wholly overshadowed any sorrow I might have felt.

I never thought I would put myself in that place again but this time even my father thought it a good match. After a brief courtship, Jonathan and I married. Within the safety of his love and care, I gradually began to realize the value of my own voice—an instrument through which I could hear my longings and demands spoken without apology. Jonathan encouraged my words, my opinions. He was a man who was well acquainted with how neglect could affect living things. It was his loving and generous heart, full of what he called "the grace of God's light" that began to fuel the beginning of my healing and the strengthening of my resolve.

Edith was born in 1923, eight months after our marriage and, of course, everyone talked. Helen came five years later, early like her sister. Things were not progressing. I was frightened. I had already lost so much.

1928

There was a time when the things I have seen I can now see no more. Everything a blur. Voices that once christened the day, offering a frantic hope, have become a staying static. When did I disappear into the noise?

A girl, another girl, but this time my husband was not disappointed. My cries met her newborn cries as I sank back. I began to feel the birth push return and grabbed Flora's arm. She smiled. I heard her say something to my husband but once released, there were only more tears, more pain, more loss.

As I lay between worlds fighting to stay but desiring to go, thoughts of Aunt Elizabeth wander through my drifting mind. I can feel her patting my hand, telling me that one day I would understand her treks through the woods as steps on her trail of prayers, that solitude breeds introspection. She said, "Even though it doesn't take long for a heart that looks inward to discover its flaws, it also opens up the possibility for redemption." I understand that now.

Words of a long-forgotten hymn float into my consciousness—*I know that for me all is well.* All is well. The well. "I'm sorry momma. I should have been better." The haze around my sight sharpens. "Is that you, Jonathan?" I hear the words, "Come to the well, and I will give you living water." I am frightened but know beyond knowing I am safe. I sink further away as He takes my hand in His.

A Hard Resolve

Edith

1923-1987

My first vivid memory was of my mother's groaning and my father rushing around our small home, stoking the stove and taking orders from the town's midwife, Flora Jane, a name spoken together by those who stood distant from her exquisite difference. I was too young to understand the root of their narrow ways, so I was free to love the deep color of her skin.

I stood just outside my parent's bedroom, clutching the broadcloth table cover, afraid of the sounds. I watched Mrs. Washington—my father insisted on the formality with us children as a sign of respect—as her confident words calmed my mother. She was a gentle woman who along with her mother had birthed more babies, including me, than the doctor who had a questionable reputation with women. Her beautiful brown hands, rough with work, were gentle and sure as they comforted my mother. Grey peppered her wiry curls, a sign of her age, of her wisdom she said.

Mrs. Washington looked up and saw my hesitance to come closer.

"Edith, come sit by your mother. She is about to bring life to your little family." When she saw me sink back, she laughed. "I understand, child. The sounds of birth can be frightening but to me they are a glorious…"

Just then my mother let out a groaning sob, and I started to cry. Flora gently held a cloth to my mother's wet forehead.

"Edith, take your sister and go get wood for the stove. We need it warm in here to keep the chill off this new life when it comes."

William, my papa's brother, who had been sitting off to the side, said to Millie and me, "Why don't we go out and get some kindling." He grabbed his cane, saying, "Get your coats and scarves. It's cold out." He nodded to Flora and smiled.

When we came back in our sister, named Helen, was being wrapped in a muslin towel and placed in a small wooden box. Flora handed the box to my father and said, "Put her near the stove. We have to keep her warm."

When he brought her out I saw her tiny form. "Papa, why is the baby going by the stove?"

"She's come too early, Edith, and she's very small. We have to keep her warm."

Just then I heard a moan from the bedroom.

"Well, look at this," said Flora as she carefully checked my mother. "Another child."

My father looked over at William and left us to watch over our new sister. He quickly went into the dimly lit room and closed the door between us. I could still hear Mrs. Washington's encouraging voice.

"Just one more push, Mary. Good. Now just rest."

The ensuing sounds confused me. Muffled words from my father and Flora. The only cry I heard was a soft weeping from my mother. A few minutes later my father appeared with a small bundle. He carried it outside without a word.

"Where's he going? Why isn't the baby crying like Helen?" I asked Mildred.

Wise beyond her years at just seven she said, "Hush now. Go sit by the stove and watch the baby."

William looked over at us and just shook his head.

Flora eventually came out holding the soiled bed linens and pulled the door closed. "Give your momma some rest now."

"But where's the baby?" I asked, confused.

She bundled the sheets into a wicker basket and came over to me. She stooped down and put her warm hands on my face.

"Looks like this one went directly to Jesus, sweet one."

That was all she said. That's all anyone said.

Just a few short weeks later my mother, weakened by the delivery, went to be with Jesus too.

We all became surrogate mothers to Helen, doting on her, trying to fill up the space that death leaves. Even though my father's faith became a staying strength to us, I held a part of myself back, fearing I too would go directly to Jesus if I yielded my will. I could never have known then that my dismissal of a deeper faith and the loss of Helen's other would scar us all anew many years later.

I grew up between my step-sister's lingering grief and Helen's contrary disposition. It was a difficult position, being in the middle, but a place where I could easily disappear.

Even though the country was what my father called "depressed," I remember those lean years fondly, mainly due to the welcoming I always found at Mrs. Washington's small home. Filled to the brim with children, grandchildren and an occasional hobo who would show up looking for a meal and a loft to sleep in, she showed me what generosity without judgment was. Being more restrained with my affections, it was difficult to follow in her footsteps, finding it easier to judge rather than accept.

The world moved into 1938 with a slow fear building behind every conversation. I suppose my father tried to shelter us by saying it was more appropriate for girls to worry about keeping a respectable home than to dwell on the outside influences of a distressed world.

That October we noticed the attention William paid Millie had become awkward, eventually leading him to move into the small work shed behind our house. One afternoon after dinner, Millie suggested they go out to the barn to see how our cow, Cassie, was doing. It was a silly question to me. Even though William was uncomfortable around animals about to give birth, he heartily agreed. He always went with Millie wherever she wanted to go. We could all see the mutual affection growing between them. It wasn't a surprise when they eventually wed, moving down the road to start their lives together. I thought it incredibly romantic.

Flora's grandson, Elijah, and his parents lived about a mile from our farm. His father had been a man who could fix anything which made him invaluable to those around us who oddly resented his skill. When he passed, those in town offered no words of comfort except to say they now needed someone to replace him. What was spoken in low tones was of the impropriety of our closeness. My father paid no heed to their offensive remarks seeing nothing inappropriate in our friendship, even encouraging it.

Helen grew to think of Elijah as a brother, someone to look up to, feel brave with. She became the sister he had always wanted and he the brother she needed. With only two years between us, Elijah and I shared a special bond. We told each other stories, ones that as we grew became safe havens for us both.

When I was younger, I didn't understand the difficulties he faced. I was confused when he said he'd wait for me outside the store or why he didn't go to school with the rest of us children. But the year I turned twelve and he fourteen after two boys beat him unconscious for walking too close to their sister did I finally understand just how the difference between us would separate and threaten.

Even though my father only gave credence to what lay beneath the skin of a man, most of those around us saw Elijah's family and those who were like them differently. Only valued for how they made most of our neighbor's lives easier, their humanity was lost in the intolerance of a community who claimed to know God. This infuriated us all, except my Uncle Andrew who grew to become a bitter voice against anyone who associated with those he considered beneath him.

Over the next few years, I didn't see much of Elijah. I was busy with home duties and completing my studies at school. I began to notice the changes not only in the members of my family but in me. When the girls at school whispered about their affections toward a particular boy, I found myself standing aloof, not sharing their enthusiasm. Whenever I thought about the kind of boy I would like, I always thought of Elijah who was kind and gentle and brave. But I kept this to myself, now understanding the great divide between us.

1939

Millie and William's wedding was a beautiful yet simple affair. They chose to be married at our home instead of the town's church. They both wanted Flora and her family to attend and knew they wouldn't be welcomed elsewhere. My father's long-time friend, a minister who was visiting from out west, performed the ceremony. He had them stand in front of our stone well as they said their vows, saying, "As you both stand before this source of life-sustaining water, be reminded of how Jesus, the Rock of our faith, encompasses those who seek to be filled with His living water." Although I didn't really understand the words, I liked the way he spoke and how welcoming he was to all our friends.

I secretly hoped Elijah would be there, but Mrs. Washington was uncertain if he would make it back in time. For the last six months he had been away, helping an uncle who was recovering from an accident.

Finally able to get away from the activities, I went down by the stream to ponder all that had happened during the ceremony and my rising feelings toward someone I knew could never be mine. The coolness of the stream relieved me. Lost in my thoughts, I didn't hear him approach until I felt his hand on my shoulder.

"Eli, you startled me!"

"Sorry, didn't mean to. Didn't want to disturb. Looked like you were deep in thought."

"I was just taking a few minutes away from everyone. When did you get back?"

"Yesterday."

"Why didn't you come see me?"

"I wasn't sure if I should; if you'd want me to."

"Why wouldn't I want to see you?" It was then I noticed a hardness on his face. He looked older, more—worn. Elijah stepped past me up to the edge of the bank. He picked up a stone and threw it at the deep part so it made a loud *thunk*.

"You seem tired. Was the work difficult?"

"The work? No. Not the work."

"Then what?"

He turned to me and said, "Edith, you have no idea…." He picked up another stone and pressed its hard surface into his palms. He threw it with such force it landed on the other side of the stream. He was getting upset with an anger I had not seen before. I moved over to him and gently touched his arm, standing closer than I ought.

Pulling away he said, "I can't...I can't see you anymore. What I'm feeling for you can get us both in trouble, maybe even get me killed!"

I stepped over to him and took his hand in mine. "Elijah, I love you, and I don't care who knows." I was becoming undone.

"Stop! We can't do this." He shook my hand from his and grasped my shoulders to push me back but couldn't. He just stared into my eyes and said, "Edith..."

I had never been kissed before. His lips were cracked from the sun but tender. Every desire we had hidden for the past year came to the surface and began to consume us.

We stayed at the stream longer than we should have, done things I'm sure we shouldn't have done, but I didn't care. We were in love, and that was all we knew. In our youthful way, we pronounced vows to each other, ones I remembered hearing at Millie's wedding. I was to be his forever.

Elijah and I would meet whenever we could. It was thrilling to steal away, to hold each other, to imagine a life free of hate and danger. But for now, we were invisible to a world that was a fading shadow.

The day before Christmas we snuck away and exchanged small tokens. He carved a tiny bird, a sparrow he said to remind me how special I was to him and to God. I gave him a poem I had written, pouring out my love for him. I didn't sign it knowing if it was found we would both be in trouble. If we had only known it was the last time we would be together, we never would have parted.

Three days later, Elijah's Uncle Joel came to our home to tell us his nephew was dead. He had been shot. Details were hazy but he was told a man was seen beating a woman in an alley, both white. A witness said Elijah and another man tried to break them up when a shot was heard. When it was over, Elijah lay dead on the street.

No arrests were made.

My father was understandably disturbed and shocked, but I was distraught beyond imagining. Everyone thought I was just grieving the loss of a dear friend but the pain was so deep it was making me sick. I couldn't sleep and everything I ate came back up. My father, worried about my continued state, said, "Edith, I'm calling the doctor. This sickness is beyond grief. "

"No, please don't get him. Ask Mrs. Washington to come."

When Flora entered my small room and saw me, she closed the door and came and sat on my bed. She gently wiped the hair away from my face and said, "Child, don't you know Elijah is where there is no pain, no sorrow, no hatred?"

Angered by her words I yelled, "But he's not with me!"

Flora, wise in the ways of the world, instantly knew the source of my pain and my sickness. She tenderly rocked me as I wept in her arms.

"Oh, dear Jesus. What have we here? A child with a child in a world where there is no pity, no love."

As soon as Flora spoke the words I pushed myself away from her. I wanted to deny the possibility but knew in that moment I was blessed and damned at the same time. She stayed with me until I fell asleep, trying to console and relieve my fears.

The next morning my father sent Helen out to the barn, saying he needed to speak with me alone. He handed me a cup of tea and sat down.

"Edith, what are we to do? You know the shame others will lay on you and the child, even more so because of who Elijah is—was."

"I don't care. Don't you see, Papa? There is a part of Elijah still here." I laid my hands on my stomach. "Here. Inside me. He'll never be completely gone now."

My father just shook his head, knowing he would not be able to reason with me while I was in this agitated state.

"Edith, Mrs. Washington made a suggestion. She has a cousin north of here who she is sure would be willing to have you come stay with her. If you are in agreement, she will write to her today and make the arrangements."

"But Papa. Leave you and Helen? And go stay with a stranger?" I began to plead with him but to no avail.

"Edith, you have to trust I know what needs to be done. Do you trust me?"

He gave me his handkerchief and laid his hand on my head. "Dear one, you will never be far from my thoughts or my love. God will get us through this. Let's pray now for His will in this matter."

Even though I closed my eyes, I could not repeat his words. I was being sent away, something shameful to be hidden and forgotten. The betrayal circled me like the stones stacked around our well. But I did not feel protected, just desolate and alone.

My father told Helen and anyone else who questioned my absence that I had gone to take care of an infirmed relative who needed my help.

Looking out the train's smudged window, I was as desolate as the landscape that flew by. The pounding ache inside matched the numbing rhythm of the wheels beneath us.

Mrs. Washington sat across from me, head nodding back sleep, hands still clutching her small bag. When harsh words and angry looks followed us to our seats, she kept her head erect and back straight. I wondered if this was what lay ahead for my child. I pushed the thought away and closed my eyes.

She stayed a few days with us before returning. "Now Edith, I don't want you to mope around and be a burden. You need to see beyond this situation and be grateful to what God is giving you. Do you understand?"

I shook my head yes, but I didn't. Not really.

Mabel Johnson was a gentle woman, dedicated to her children and her husband, a man I wasn't certain approved of my presence in his home. Mabel dismissed my concerns saying it was "Just his way."

Life soon fell into a pleasing rhythm where I tried to move past my pain and into what lay ahead. My time was spent helping Mabel with the sewing she took in. A gifted seamstress, she was quietly admired by those she worked for. I also helped look after her three children, three girls aged five, seven, and ten.

Mabel's fifteen-year-old son, Simon, had taken a job with the railroad and was rarely home. At first her eldest daughter, Harriet, stood apart from me but it wasn't long before she realized I was not there to order or replace. Because she preferred working outdoors to threading a needle, most days her mother put her to work in their bountiful garden. I learned from both of them—mending and growing, something I had always resisted.

The months rushed by, my days filled with pleasant companionship and purpose. In the evenings once the children were asleep and her husband was situated on the porch with his pipe, Mabel would often tell me stories about her family, stories of heartbreak and endurance in the face of overwhelming intolerance and hate, of how her grandparents were forced to leave their home and community to make room so "rich white folks could have more room to picnic."

I knew I'd never truly understand her pain. When I told her I was sorry for how awful people could be, she was silent for a while and then said, "Edith, saying you're sorry is just a beginning that takes a person's whole life to make into action. But what we're doing here? Sharing, loving each other? I'd say you are well on your way."

"But how can you ever forgive..." I winced at the thought of forgiveness so grand in the face of such brutality. I thought about my own pain, my own unforgiveness toward the one who shot Elijah, even toward my father who sent me away. All I could say was, "Mabel, how?"

She came and sat down next to me and took my hand. "Child, forgiveness don't mean forgetting. It simply means choosing to cut the chain that binds to the one who caused the hurt."

Mabel stood and went over to the room where her children slept. She put her hand on the door and gently stroked it. She turned and said in a quiet but forceful voice, "But for me, I've had *enough* of chains."

The magnitude of her grace inspired and shamed me at the same time.

My somewhat cloistered life with Mabel allowed me to begin to repair the torn parts of my life. The few neighbors who occasionally stopped by usually just shook their heads when they first saw me. All were met with Mabel's firm belief that we were all children of the same God. None saw fit to argue.

Toward the end of my time, Mabel sat me down and had a serious conversation. "Edith, I was wanting to have this talk with you for some time now. I'll speak plainly. What do you plan on doing once the child comes?"

"Do? Well, I thought we'd go back home to my father."

Her expression changed, became solemn. "You know this child will not…not look the way…will look different."

I could tell she struggled with her words, struggled to tell me something I was unwilling to hear. I closed my eyes and wistfully said, "I know I'm naïve, but I hope the child is just like Elijah."

Mabel winced at my inexperience and my adolescent ideas. "That's a mite selfish, don't you think?"

I got up and stood behind the chair and pressed my fingers into the wood. Her words made me uneasy, unsettled my resolve. Deep inside I knew the words she spoke were meant for my good, for my child's good.

Mabel smiled and motioned for me to sit back down. Obediently, I did as I was told.

"Edith, you can't really know the lot we bear in this life. Even though your father looks beneath a man's skin, most others don't. And this child will have it even harder, not being one or the other."

My ignorance silenced me. My mind was brought back to Mabel's stories of the harsh and cruel treatment her people had endured. I thought about Elijah lying dead at the hands of a white man who would never see a day in jail. "Oh, Mabel. What should I do? I could never stand it if my child was hurt."

Mabel took my hands in hers and said, "I've spoken to my husband and he agrees that the best place for this child is here with us." She immediately saw my misgivings and said, "I know, I know he's a mite standoffish, but he's a good man. Just awkward with his feelings is all. He's been through a lot, lost a lot in this life. I don't want you to answer me right now. Take some time. Pray on it and see what the good Lord would have you do."

I thanked her and went outside to walk and to think. Mabel didn't know I wasn't much for praying, but because I knew she understood life in a way I never could, I took her words to heart and considered her offer.

The pains began in the middle of the night. As they intensified, I got up not wanting to disturb the children whose room I shared. I grabbed a small blanket and quietly snuck out to the porch. The night's chill eased me, at least for the first hour. Every time the pain returned, I looked up into the sky, trying to fix my eyes on a star, focus on the dim light. "Oh Eli," I said softly, "Can you see me? Do you know your child will be born soon? Without you?" Unable to contain my hurt, I started to softly weep.

I didn't hear the door open or see John, Mabel's husband, approach.

"What you doing out here in the middle of the night?"

"I'm sorry if I disturbed you. I was having some pain and didn't want to wake the children."

"Pain, huh. So it's your time then."

I responded with new tears. "I'm sorry. I'm just scared."

He was silent for a minute then came and sat next to me. "It's natural to be scared. Mabel was scared with all four of our children, even cried some too. Nothing to be shamed over."

I did not expect this show of kindness. "Thank you for understanding." Just then another pain, one stronger than the others, came on me. I groaned louder than I intended.

"I think it's time to go inside and get Mabel."

As I stood, water poured out from me. I looked at John about to apologize but he just smiled and said, "Yup. Time to get Mabel."

Later the next day, my daughter was born, with dark curls crowning her small head and skin the beautiful color of wet sand.

"Oh, Mabel, she's wonderful."

As she gathered the soiled bed linens she said, "That she is. What you gonna name her?"

"Can I really name her?"

"Seems fitting to me."

My daughter squirmed and made a small cry. Mabel came and sat next to me.

"Here. Let me help get you both started. There's no milk yet, but it gets her used to where she can get it." She discreetly showed me how to offer my breast. "It'll take some practice, but you'll both do fine."

I was embarrassed but welcomed her help. Looking at my daughter's sweet face I tried to imagine a name that would suit her features and honor her father. As if offering up a prayer I breathed out, "Esther."

"Esther?

"The name just came to me. Not sure from where. I like the sound of it. From the Bible I think."

She smiled. "There's a whole book about Esther." Mabel smoothed the quilt as she spoke. "Esther was a very brave woman. Because she did what was right her people were saved." Standing she said, "Esther is a worthy name, one I'm certain Elijah would have liked."

I looked down at my daughter again, soon not to be my daughter and said, "Esther it is."

Just then there was a soft knock at the door. It creaked open and ten-year-old Harriet poked her head in.

"Can we come in?

I nodded to Mabel who went to the door and said, "All right everyone. Come meet your new baby sister."

The three girls all crowded around me fawning over the new life I held in my arms. When Esther began to cry, Anne reached over and tried to soothe her.

When she said, "It's okay, baby. Don't cry. It's your birthday," I began to feel myself fall away.

Mabel noticed and said, "Edith, why don't I take the baby so you can get some rest?"

I nodded weakly and thanked her.

Mabel took Esther and wrapped her in a small quilt. "Let's give the new mother some time to rest."

But was I a mother? And if I wasn't, what was I?

I stayed with Mabel and her family for six months until Esther was able to be weaned. Attached to my daughter through her need, the closeness this brought only deepened the ache of knowing it would soon end. Mabel mostly left us alone, except to share her wisdom when needed. I listened to everything she said cherishing this time not only with my daughter but with a woman who had become like a mother to me. I watched her children already behaving like Esther was just another sibling to fawn over. This pleased but saddened me knowing I would soon have to leave this unexpected refuge.

When the agreed upon day arrived, I fell apart. All the emotions I had held within me came tumbling out as John put my bag in his old truck to take me to the train.

"I can't do this. I just can't leave her." Mabel's tight embrace brought me back to the comfort and safety her cousin once encircled me with.

"Now, now. You can do this because you love your daughter and because you loved Elijah. You know this is best and because mothers always do the best for their children you will get on that train. Oh, you'll never forget that she is...she was yours. You need to choose to let Jesus hold that part of your heart so it doesn't get hard. Will you promise me you'll do that?"

"I promise." I had never lied directly to someone's face before that day, but the moment the train began to move, the small center of my once malleable heart became a hard resolve that shaped the next forty years of my life.

Helen

1928-1992

I never said I knew. I had noticed Edith and Elijah sneaking off when our father was busy and unaware, but I never said anything, figured they just didn't want me along. When Edith went away that winter, Papa said she was going to help out a relative I had never heard of. When I asked more, he just said, "Your sister is going where she needs to go."

When Edith returned, she was different. She was—vacant. She disappeared a lot which bothered me but worried my father. Once I found her by the stream motionless, looking straight ahead. All of a sudden, she picked up a rock and threw it. As I came up beside her, I noticed how intently she watched the disappearing ripples.

"Edith, what are you doing?"

Still staring into the water she said, "Did you ever wonder where they go? The ripples? They just fade away, like they were never there." She bent down and picked up another stone. Suddenly angry, she turned toward me and raised it as if to throw it at me. "Helen! Stop bothering me! Can't you see I need some time to myself?" Edith turned back toward the stream and threw the stone so hard it bounced off a rock and shattered.

"You *always* need time for yourself these days."

"You don't understand. You're too young."

"I'm not too young!" Thinking I knew what bothered her I said, "I miss Elijah too; so does Papa. That's no reason to be so, so…I don't know what!" I started to tear up but refused to cry.

Edith looked at me but past me. She gave a halting smile. "I'm sorry, Helen. I know you miss him."

"I miss you too."

Her hardness faded. "Come on. Let's go back and see if your Miss Kitty has given birth yet." She took my hand like she used to and led me home.

Tucked into one of the corners of the stall, my favorite cat was cleaning her three newly-born kittens. I approached quietly so as not to startle her. Edith hung back by the door.

Motioning, I quietly said, "Come in. See. She might let you pick one up. Just can't take it from her sight."

"No. I'll stay here. We don't want to overwhelm the new mother."

I thought Edith had grown too mature to find delight in a simple kitten but later that week I came into the barn and found her cradling one of the babies, softly singing over its little form. There was something desperate in the way she held it. When my father insisted we give them away saying there were enough cats around the farm already, she shouted, "How could you!" and ran off in tears.

I tried to go after her but he stopped me saying, "Leave her be, Helen. Leave her be."

I found her at the stream again, just staring. The tension between us had been taut, about to snap. I usually left her alone but this time I came up behind her and roughly tapped her shoulder. "Edith, I'm tired of doing my work *and* yours! You do less and less every day."

"Helen, just leave me alone! You don't understand. You'll never understand!"

The words I spoke next defined the course of our relationship for years to come. As she turned to go, I grabbed her arm. "You think I don't know where you went and why?"

Edith turned sharply. "What? What did Papa say to you?"

“He didn’t say anything. I saw how you and Elijah would sneak away. I even saw you kissing one time.”

“Kissing? We were just...playing. You need to mind your own business.”

I could see she was getting upset, but I couldn’t stop. I then said what I thought I’d never say. “I heard Papa and Mrs. Washington talking. They sent me outside, but I came back and listened by the window. It was open and I heard Papa say, ‘Flora, what am I to do? Edith doesn’t understand what this means, doesn’t understand what having Elijah’s baby would mean to her or the child.’”

The look on Edith’s face told me I never should have spoken. My words just came rushing out, a current meant to push. “See, I know your secret. You had a baby and left it somewhere!”

Edith turned and faced me full. There were tears pooling in her eyes but her mouth was pressed tight as if holding back her words. She crossed her arms and hugged herself, walking over to the water’s edge. The wind picked up and lifted her hair, tossed it against the side of her face. She stood there, silent with her back straight and rigid. The only sound was the water lapping against the small rocks that littered the sand. Pine-scented air swirled around us both, a fragrance wasted on the moment.

After a few very long minutes she said, “Secrets? Well, I know a secret too, Helen.” She turned and rushed at me, standing just a few inches from my face. “Bet you didn’t know you probably killed our brother and maybe even momma.”

She could tell by my shocked look that her arrows had hit their mark.

“You take that back! I did no such thing. We never had a brother!” I pushed her away, pushed her words away.

She smirked. "Just after you were born I heard Mrs. Washington say there was another child coming. The next thing I knew Papa came out of their bedroom with a small bundle. No crying baby, just a lifeless form that now lies with momma."

"You're lying! I'm going to tell Papa!"

"Go ahead. Hurt him too."

She turned and ran back toward the house. I stayed at the stream for a long time, trying to understand what she said. Could it be true? Or was that just something she said to hurt me? But she was right. I couldn't ask my father. If it was true, I had already done enough damage.

We never spoke of the harsh words spoken that day. I tried to once but knew it would be no use—the Edith I knew was gone.

After consulting with the doctor, it was decided to send her away for a time to a school, a place where he said the fresh air could help her heal and recover. He refused to detail what she needed to recover from, just said her grief had made her heart sullen. When she returned, it was clear the hardness that had framed her face that day at the stream had taken root, isolating her from all of us.

One month later, Edith moved in with our great-aunt Elizabeth, becoming caretaker to her aging and to the cabin by the lake.

1941

Life returned to a stilted normal after Edith left. My father's unspoken heartache framed our days, cloistered us against the world's conflict that threatened to intrude at any moment. The threat of war framed every conversation, fed every doubt about the future.

We all held our breath when a distant enemy dropped bombs into paradise and threatened our country's eminence. The exhale took years as we collectively watched and prayed for those who faced unimaginable devastation, loss of ethnic identity, and death. Even though we were somewhat sheltered in the tentative security of our rural community, we still knew the grief of lost sons, fathers and brothers. I felt the sting but selfishly focused on how the inconveniences and shortages of war affected me.

We heard from Edith once when she coldly informed us of our aunt's death. She said there would be no service as Elizabeth wanted to be quietly buried near her home. That was all. When Papa asked if she would come home, even visit, she just replied, "The cabin was left to me. I'm fine where I am."

The years created a distance between me and my father. I wanted to believe it was just his way, not knowing how to handle an irritable daughter. He spent his days tending animals and giving comfort to those around us who lost loved ones in the war. His sensitive heart and ardent faith gave him the words needed to soothe.

It was during this time he met Margaret, a widow whose son died even before going overseas when the car he was driving overturned after a night of drinking. Each with their own brand of loss, they found a binding strength in each other's company. Margaret was kind, tried her best to give me what neither of us knew I needed. But even with all of their attempts at making me feel included, a strange jealousy began to form in me after they were married, making me even more difficult to be around. I dropped into my teenage years, a tossed stone, spreading out from the depth of my insecurity like ripples in stagnant water.

1945

The cancer that ate away at Margaret not only threatened the heart of my father's faith but derailed my hope of finally leaving behind the dull predictability of my life. Stronger than my love for my father was the need to get away, out from under the heaviness I carried.

Margaret died on the day we dropped our bombs on the enemy who dropped their bombs on us, signaling the beginning of a devastation that would change the way the world fought. I had read that the explosion left shadows of those caught in its wake, something I understood. I searched as one lost to find the life I imagined I deserved.

We had known Frank's father, a blacksmith, for years. From time to time he would come to our farm to shoe our three horses. He didn't stay, embarrassed by his thick Italian accent. Frank's mother, a straightforward woman who shared her son's uneven features, never shied away from others. She didn't seem embarrassed over her awkward speech or the noticeable bump in her nose, irregular teeth and small eyes; in fact, it appeared to me she wore her imperfections like a badge hard won. I admired the way she carried herself, a woman on a mission, eyes forward, no looking back.

Even then Frank and I had a lot in common. He, after serving in the army and fighting for what I was told was my freedom, had been stuck waiting, waiting overseas while American politicians and dissenting communists vied for control. I, too, had been stuck. I was a willful adolescent of sixteen when he left to serve but now almost two years later I was waiting, waiting for something, someone to carry me away from a place where, like Frank, I believed I lost my life.

1946

I decided to fall in love with Frank in of all places—church. I had just turned eighteen and had a plan in place to leave that wouldn't devastate or anger my father.

On a cool Sunday morning in September I lingered outside of our small church for as long as possible, talking with a few friends who also wanted to linger. An old car pulled up, backfiring once when turned off. This sent my friends and me into uncontrollable laughter. I watched as Frank got out and politely offered his mother a hand. He glanced over toward our group, hearing the commotion. As his eyes met mine he gave me a slight smile. When I returned his attention my friends made an even bigger scene.

"Helen, what are you doing?" asked my friend, Muriel. "That's just Frank Martin. At least that's what he calls himself." Muriel leaned in close and whispered, "Shirley told me when his parents came to America they changed their names. His real last name is Marconi or something strange like that. To try and fit in I guess." She looked back at Frank, tossed her curls and said, "He's so...different and not handsome in the least."

I glared at Muriel. "Well, I think he's interesting looking. We better go in or our fathers will go crazy." We joined arms and walked up the steps. I looked back and our eyes met. He smiled again, and I turned red.

Frank was tall, lanky some would say, with uneven features that unsettled those who looked for perfection. Even though he had a noticeable scar which could be seen above his collar, I was immediately drawn to him, mysterious enough to pique my interest, available enough to aid in my plan.

That next Sunday I suggested to my father we invite him to dinner, feigning patriotic duty to a returning soldier. At first

Frank was reluctant, embarrassed by the attention. But after my father said his parents were, of course, also invited, he agreed. So later that day the man who I was certain would rescue me came to our house and into my life.

Frank had returned from overseas, broken in his eyes, but more than enough in mine. Even though he had a serious nature, one opposite than mine, we got along. After that first dinner, I pursued his attention, delighting him but alarming my father.

One afternoon after our usual Sunday dinner I pulled him aside, away from prying eyes. "Frank, let's just the two of us take a ride. It's such a beautiful day."

When he hesitated I said, "You just bought that snazzy car. Don't you want to take it for a spin?" Frank was very proud of his new purchase. Something good, he said, to come out of the war.

I leaned into him and touched his face a little too close to his scar. I could tell he was uncomfortable, so I moved my hand down to his arm, giving him a knowing smile. I could feel his muscles relax.

He gently pulled me closer and said, "Where do you want to go?"

I hesitated but knew this might be a way of bringing Frank into a past I had avoided. "My father told me and my sister stories when we were younger, stories my mother shared with him about a cabin up near Watley's Lake where she visited as a child. Her aunt, Elizabeth Crandell, lived there until she died. It's been on my mind a lot lately."

"You and your sister? Your father mentioned once that his other daughter was currently living elsewhere, but I don't believe I've ever heard you talk about her."

A silent panic rose up. Uncertain over the uneasiness that came with my words, I tried to sound casual. "I haven't seen her for a long time. We had…words many years ago and haven't spoken since." I left it at that, not wanting, like Frank, to dredge up past pains.

My father was taken aback when I told him Frank and I wanted to take a drive up to the lake and look for the cabin. But as usual when faced with anything uncomfortable or inconsistent regarding my behavior, he simply acquiesced and gave us directions.

We drove for a few hours, winding over small roads and through even smaller towns. As we pulled up to the worn sign announcing we had arrived Frank said, "Do you know where the cabin is? There's a few places scattered around." Just then we saw an old man, slanted with age, walking with an old dog down the dirt road.

"Let's ask him if he's still alive by the time we get there" I said jokingly. We pulled up alongside him.

"Good afternoon, sir," Frank said politely. "We're looking for Elizabeth Crandell's cabin. We…"

I interrupted, impatient with Frank's courtesy. "Did you know her? It would have been a long time ago. My sister, Edith, lived there for a while. Maybe you knew her too."

The old man looked intently at me, making me suddenly embarrassed by the ruby red lipstick I applied after I left my father.

His condescending gaze stopped at Frank. His finger pointed with his words. "Got that in the war? Got one of those myself."

"Sir?" asked Frank.

He pointed to the puckered skin around Frank's collar and shirtsleeve. "One of them there souvenirs…from the war." He pulled up his shirt to show us a scar that had shriveled along with his age. "Got mine in the Great War, though wasn't too great for those of us who were there." He chuckled as he lowered his shirt. "Where'd you get yours?"

Frank pulled on his collar. "Oh, well, um…" Frank lowered his eyes, then said, "Something I don't like to talk about if you don't mind, sir."

I could tell Frank was becoming anxious so I said, "Excuse me, but do you know where the cabin is?"

My question drew his attention from Frank. "Miss Crandell? Yeah, I knew her. Built our cabin a few years after hers. Ours is 'bout a mile and a half down that way." He lifted his arm and pointed, showing age and fragility, making me even more uncomfortable.

"Yup, we had quite a little spread. Had chickens, some goats. Gracie, that's my wife, had a garden others wished they had. We had a nice life. Least until I was taken for the war. Them was hard years for my Grace, but she stayed strong, stayed here waitin' for me." As he talked, he began to fade, his eyes re-seeing a time long gone. "Yup, me and my wife, Grace, lived there. At least until…"

"Excuse me" I interrupted and repeated the question he ignored. "Do you know where the cabin is?" Frank could tell by my tone I was getting impatient. He tried to settle me by putting his hand on mine, but I just pulled away not wanting to be settled.

The old man looked at me like he just saw me and said, "She was a good woman, she was, a teacher I recollect. Stayed on even when her man died. Weren't even married yet. Shame it was. He didn't even get a chance to live in what his hands had built. Told my Gracie she felt him there."

He shifted his attention to his dog, bent down to grab a small stick and threw it. "Yup. Her and my wife got along real good. Grace even gave her some chickens and taught her everything she knew about keeping up a good garden, too.

Never really knew your sister. Saw her a couple times, though. Kept to herself. Pretty but not too friendly. Nope, not at all. Stayed a while after Elizabeth passed, then just up and left." His mouth closed tight into a shrunken grin calling attention to his lack of teeth and his age. He bent down to pet his dog, appearing to have forgotten my question.

"Sir, the cabin?" When he didn't respond, I thought perhaps he didn't hear me. "Excuse me, but..."

"I heard ya, young lady. I heard ya." He smirked just enough to aggravate me. "Just wondering why you want to see the old place. Think someone bought it. Not sure though. Not my business."

Someone bought it? I raised my voice and said, "All we want is to see it. Can you help us or not?" Frank looked over at me, surprised at my impatient tone, but I didn't care.

The old man ignored me and spoke directly to Frank. "The cabin is the last one down that way maybe a mile or so. Road gets pretty rough, though. Better be careful not to go too fast. There's a mighty sharp bend half way down. You young people don't have much sense these days. "

Knowing I was getting ready for an argument, Frank put his hand on my shoulder and said, "Thanks for the directions, old timer. We appreciate your help."

Frank gave a wave and carefully pulled away, not wanting to kick up dirt and stone, he said, didn't want to appear ungrateful. We travelled around half a mile or so when we came to the bend, almost driving off the road. I closed my eyes and screamed, "Frank!" He reached out and patted my hand.

"We're okay. Boy, that old man wasn't kidding about the turn. Hate to take it when the roads are slick."

Calming down I said, "They should put up a sign or something. Someone could get killed."

"Guess there's not enough traffic here to make it worth it. Not too many live around here." He pointed to a small cabin tucked into the trees. "There. That must be it. Last one. Road ends here." Once Frank stopped the car, he just sat there.

"Frank, are you getting out?"

"Feels like we're intruding here."

"That's ridiculous. We're just looking."

"Maybe, but that's how I'm feeling. You go. I'll be along in a minute."

Opening the car door I said, "Fine. I'll go myself. That's what I always do anyway." I slammed the door which sounded louder than it should have against the stillness of the pines. Leaving Frank's indecision behind, I made my way alone. My heart began to race, an erratic beat that threatened to pound my resolve.

As I stood before the neglected cabin, tears began to form. The boarded up windows closed off the past, a final warning—come no further. Just as I was rethinking the wisdom of coming, I felt a reassuring hand on my shoulder.

"Quite an old place. A shame to have let it go. I bet it was something when it was first built. When was that?"

I wiped my eyes before Frank could notice and said, "Well, let's see. Must have been built around 1870 something, not really sure. My father told us the story of how our great aunt's fiancé died a week after he had finished building the cabin. Was to be a wedding present. Not sure how he died, though. My father was unsure himself. But it left Elizabeth alone and heartbroken. Despite her parents' urging, she moved into the cabin and that's where she lived until she died. At least that's the story."

Frank took my hand, and we walked around to the back. "This is really something," he said. "I'd love to fix a place like this up some day. Would make a great place for us to come in the summer, don't you think?"

That was the first time I heard Frank refer to him and me as *us*. I turned to face him and boldly leaned in to kiss him.

"What was that for?"

"Oh, I just wanted you to know I like being referred to as *us*."

He smiled and held me close. His embrace made me feel protected, made me believe I really did love him.

I must have put my hand a little too close to his collar because he suddenly pulled back.

"Are you okay?"

"Sure." He gently held both my hands and said, "Want to go down by the lake?"

"You go. I'll be there is a minute." Relieved, he gave me a brief kiss and headed down the trail. As I walked around the graying timbers, I was pulled into a past I swore I'd never revisit. *Edith lived here.*

The wind began to pick up, sending the subtle scent of pine and renewed accusations. Tears threatened as I ran down the small trail toward Frank. I found him skipping a stone into the water.

He turned and smiled. "Hey there. Thought you got lost."

I ran over and pulled him to me, hard, wanting to push out everything else.

"Are you alright?"

"I'm fine. I just got a chill."

He stood behind me and circled me with his arms. "You're shivering." He held me closer as we faced the water. "I could stay here forever. Couldn't you?"

I closed my eyes against it all and said, "I could stay anywhere as long as you were there with me." I was glad he wasn't able to see my face. A part of me believed what I said, the part of me who still wanted redemption. When it all became too much for me, I told Frank I was getting cold and it was time to leave.

Later that week I told my father Frank and I were to be married.

He cautioned me, "Helen, I've noticed once in a while Frank has…sullen moods. I've seen many who've come back from the war carrying a heaviness about them." I could tell my father was uncomfortable. When I started to interrupt him, he put his hand on my shoulder and led me over to the chair. "Please. Sit." He sat next to me and leaned in. "I know you've heard that Millie's father died when she was just a baby." He paused and said, "Helen, this is to stay between us. Millie doesn't need to know what's said here."

Because I, more than most, understood the need to keep hurtful secrets close I nodded my agreement.

"Thank you. But what you don't know is that the man your mother was married to before me was…not a good man. He was harsh, cruel even. Now I'm not saying Frank is anything like him or would ever hurt you, but I'd like you to stop and think before marrying him. Time will tell me—you whether it's a good match. Maybe wait until next year."

"Next year? No. I'm done waiting." I got up to leave, smoothed my skirt and said firmly, "Frank is a good man who loves me. I will marry him with or without your blessing."

My father knew he'd lose me if he tried to keep me from Frank so he conceded, offering to help us build a small house on our property. Even though Frank thought it a good idea, I declined saying we'd rather move closer to town, closer to a more lively life, further away from the memories my home held.

The ceremony was a simple affair appropriate for the times. After we married, we moved to a small but thriving town about thirty miles southeast of our families. Frank was uncomfortable leaving his parents, but I convinced him we needed to begin our life together where opportunity and prosperity would ensure a happy future.

Because Frank had saved most of his wages during the war, we were able to rent a small house and live comfortably until he found a job as a mechanic at the local gas station, a job he enjoyed. He once told me he sometimes preferred machines over people. Easier to fix, he said.

A month after we moved in, Frank began pacing the floor at night, robbing me of the sleep I not only needed physically but emotionally. I know I should have understood, been more sympathetic but the only words I had for him were, "Frank, stop it and go to bed!"

I discovered I was pregnant after one of Frank's episodes left him without a job. I insisted he see a doctor when he spent two weeks barely eating and sleeping.

After a lengthy examination, the doctor called me in. Frank was more withdrawn than ever as I sat down next to him. "Helen, I've talked to Frank about all this, but he wanted me to discuss it with you."

I turned to my husband. "Frank?" His face a silhouette, one side framed by his scar which looked more pronounced, made deeper by his apparent anguish.

The doctor's voice brought me around. "Helen, I've seen more than my share of this." He motioned with his head toward a depleted Frank. "Men who can't move on, whose experiences seem to burrow deep." He fiddled with some papers on his desk and adjusted his seat, seeming just as uncomfortable as my husband. "Helen, I've given Frank a prescription to help him sleep. I also told him he should find something he enjoys doing, something that makes him feel—useful. Frank? Come back in a few weeks and we'll talk again. All right?"

Frank barely lifted his head and said, "Sure thing, Doc. Sure." We left the office, silence between us like another person.

Later that week we visited my father, something Frank suggested.

"I'm going to go out to the barn and see your father. The animals seem to ease me."

"Fine. Whatever you need." As I watched him disappear through the barn doors, I could finally breathe. I know I needed to support my husband but all I could think was what it meant for me. Who would support me?

Frank was unable to hold down a steady job, so we were eventually forced to move in with my father. He welcomed us, of course, making Frank feel less a failure and me more like the wayward child returning home.

1947

Mary Agnes, born on Easter, was named after a mother I never knew and Frank's mother whom I often felt compared to. Giving my first daughter their names somehow made up for the tragedy of my birth and the disappointment of Frank's expectations. I know he tried to see beyond my shortcomings as a wife and create between us what he had seen between his parents but for some reason his trying only made me less willing. Instead of being supportive during his occasional dour moods, I found myself increasingly irritated. The heaviness I married to get away from followed me, surrounded me like a shroud waiting for its corpse.

When Mary was four months old the tension in the house was at a tipping point. One day after another one of my outbursts, my father told me he and Frank might go up and see the cabin.

The suggestion infuriated me. "Elizabeth's cabin? That old thing? We don't even know who owns it now anyway. And if you two think you're going to just leave me here while…"

When I started to go off on one of my rants, my father came closer and lifted his hand, palm to me, and held it there, knowing it would silence me.

"Helen, stop." He kept his voice low. "Helen, in case you haven't noticed, Frank needs something to make him feel—something."

His words bristled but their truth shamed me. I exhaled the words, "But the cabin?"

My father sat down and patted the chair next to him. "Sit, please." I was uncomfortable sensing where this might lead, but did as I was told.

"The past few years I've been going up to the cabin just to check on it."

"What? Why didn't you say anything?" I then asked the question I didn't want an answer to. "Did you…see Edith?"

A brief, curt *no* was all the answer he was going to give. He shifted and said, "You don't know this but after I received the note from Edith informing me of Elizabeth's death I went up there to see if I could get your sister to come home." My father turned from me, his voice almost a whisper. "When I got there I discovered she had already moved out."

I found myself unsettled at the mention of her name. My father faced me again as he dabbed at his eyes.

"Your mother used to tell me all about Aunt Elizabeth's cabin in the woods. She said it was a place of possibility and promises, although she admitted her promises were often weak and forgotten." He shifted again and said, "A few days later I received the deed to the cabin in the mail."

"The deed? From Edith? Why didn't you say…?"

"It wasn't anything that needed your attention *or* your permission."

I hesitated to ask but I needed to know. "Was there a note with it?"

As he started to stand he said, "A note? Yes. Just a brief one that said she wanted to honor Elizabeth's wishes for the cabin to be passed on to someone in the family…to hold until such a time as it was..." His look darkened with every word. His words became forceful. "That it was *my* decision what to do with it."

He hesitated, turned to me and said, "Edith also wrote I was not to try and find her. That distance was profitable for all of us."

My father appeared to age as he spoke. As for me? The hollow place inside I'd lived with for years deepened with an ache beyond words.

Changing the mood he said, "I haven't done much to the place, but I think it's time. Could be good for Frank and me." I could tell he had settled things in his mind. "Of course, you are welcome to come, too. I just figured that the rough accommodations wouldn't suit you and Mary."

He knew me so well.

So every weekend the two of them left, pats on the back, tools in hand. Frank's father even joined them a few times, pleased to be included. Even though there was a part of me that resented being excluded, I was relieved when they left.

For months I had avoided visits from my mother-in-law. Her ease with Mary only made me feel like more of a failure. The last time she came, she brought a small bottle of her homemade wine. When she handed it to me, she stroked my hair. I sometimes had trouble understanding her but even with her broken English I knew it was to "help with my sadness." If she only could have known how those first drinks would cloud me for years to come.

Three months later, Frank and my father came home from the lake and pronounced the cabin "Done."

Frank beamed. "It's simple, still rugged but beautiful, Helen. A place we can go, maybe get a small rowboat too. Take both of you on the lake, maybe fish even." He handed a paper to me.

"What's this?"

"Your father signed over the deed to the cabin to you—to both of us."

Looking for something to complain about, I handed him back the paper and said, "You know Edith might show up. I couldn't handle…"

Frank looked at me and smiled. "Helen, let's not borrow trouble." He put his arms around me and said, "For now, let's just enjoy the blessing that it is."

For whatever reason I hated to admit that the cabin and the times at the lake were a reprieve from the weight I carried at my father's. Why couldn't I just "enjoy the blessing" as Frank put it?

But the gnawing discontent that was my daily shadow only worsened when Genevieve and Frank Jr. were born just two years after Mary. The more others doted on the children the more detached I felt to everything around me.

My world got even smaller when one day Frank came home to tell me he traded in our two-door for a more family-friendly four-door. Said it was safer, more stable, a better fit. *Did he even know who he married*?

As a way to ease my deepening melancholy, my father and Frank willingly took over what should have been my responsibilities, leaving me even more desolate at my apparent inability to see beyond myself.

Life fell into a cyclical rhythm, a numb routine that was predictable and safe for Frank, but regrettable for me.

1951

I began to notice my father struggling with even simple tasks. My frustration shamed me, knowing I should be concerned instead of aggravated. His labored breathing and relentless cough grated on my nerves, weakening my already fragile resolve. I was consistently overwhelmed with three small children and resented the attention Frank paid my father.

I had just gotten the twins down for a nap when I heard my father's frail voice call from his bedroom. "Helen, come in here, please."

"What is it? I need to start dinner before the children wake up." I know I was brusque and immediately regretted it when I saw my father's face.

"Please. Sit beside me." He patted the quilt and managed a weak smile "Helen, I've already talked this over with Frank. I've decided to sell most of the land and all of the animals. It's too much for me and with Frank working at the gas station again and…well, here when he gets home. It's the right decision."

An uncomfortable guilt began to stir. "Papa…"—a name I hadn't used since I was a child.

He reached out to touch my hand to silence me. "Mr. James down the road has always admired my horses, so when I approached him about the animals, he quickly agreed, even wanted the chickens. Frank asked around to see if there was anyone who might be interested in buying the ten acres across the road, and he found a Mr. Dolson, I think his name is. He says he plans on building houses, says for returning servicemen and their families, although I don't think that's his real motive." He let out a short laugh before a coughing fit overtook him.

"Let me get you some water." I started to get up but he grasped my arm, gently but with a desperate force that alarmed me. He let go and nodded, unable to catch his breath. When I came back into the room, I noticed small red spots on the handkerchief he had used to cover his mouth.

I pointed. "What's this?" I knew my tone sounded more like an accusation than a concern but weakness of any kind just distressed me.

"Nothing—nothing." He folded the cloth and feebly reached for the water. "Thank you, Helen." After taking a few small sips he said, "Just coughed too hard is all."

I sat on the end of the bed, just far enough away without offending.

"Helen, I hope you don't feel I'm selling your home out from under you. When I die, the house and insurance money will be yours and Frank's. I'll put a little something away for Edith…" My father shifted, sank back into his pillows. "The right thing to do. I just want to…"

"Stop. Please." I stood and walked over to the window, not wanting him to see my face. "This will always be *your* home. You can do as you please with it. I appreciate you letting us come here, really, but…" I turned and forced a smile. I went over to the bed and took his hand. "We'll be fine. Really." But I knew we'd be anything but fine.

After he got the children to bed, Frank spent evenings sitting at my father's bedside, reading from his Bible—my father becoming less and Frank oddly becoming more. In addition to his work as a mechanic, he began to sketch, something, he said, he had done when he was younger but had dismissed during the war. The first time he showed me one of his drawings, I was impressed but secretly jealous he had found a pleasure that was wholly his.

I took the picture from him. “Frank, this is beautiful.” It was a scene of snow-capped mountains and a glistening lake done simply with colored pencils. He had drawn in a small cabin surrounded by tall pines. “Did you draw this from memory?”

He was pleased by my compliment but looked uneasy. “No. I saw it on a calendar once. Always remembered it.”

When I said we’d have to have it framed and put it in the living room for all to appreciate he said, “Nah, just something I like to do for myself.”

When I started to object he took the picture back and started to walk out of the room. “Frank? What’s the matter? Frank?” His silence told me to let it go, but I needed an answer to at least one of my questions. I followed him into our bedroom and found him just sitting on the edge of the bed weeping. Unable to find the words needed, I closed the door and let him be.

During that time my father was desperate to contact Edith. Between spasms of pain and the drugged haze prescribed by his doctor, he wrote letters, sending them to surrounding towns in hopes of finding her. Every time he gave me one to mail I saw a faint hope well up in him, but when they started coming back stamped *address unknown* he shrank right before my eyes.

“Here, Helen. Mail this for me, please?” His hand shook as he handed me the envelope.

“Why do you do this to yourself? We don’t even know if she’s still…” Even I couldn’t finish the sentence.

“She is. I can feel she’s out there. We’ll find her. We will. This will be the last letter. I promise.”

The promise was kept when he died two days later.

Standing in the small family plot that housed my mother, Margaret, and Millie, gone three years now, buried beside her infant daughter, I felt an uncomfortable loss. Her husband, William, stood beside me leaning on his cane, silent and distraught. I stood stiff, taut from the guilt of this needed release and the shame of my vacant grief.

At the end of the small service, Frank took my hand and led me over to William who was now standing before his wife's grave. Knowing more about expressing sympathy than I did, Frank gently put his hand on William's shoulder. "Will, you know you can come stay with us. The children love you. It would be good for all of us."

"Thank you, Frank, Helen. That means a lot. But I've decided to start fresh, out west somewhere. Maybe near my cousin." William bent down and laid a few wildflowers on the hard dirt. His face had grown weary these past years. He stood up firm, straightening his shoulders. Returning to his thoughts he said, "He went west years ago. Ended up in California. I received a letter from him when Millie passed. You know, I've always wanted to see the ocean."

His eyes became distant, already seeing another sunset, and like me, already searching the horizon for meaning.

I met Ernest one week after the funeral. I was walking to my car when we almost collided as I came around the corner of the market. I dropped one of my bags and as we both leaned over to pick it up we bumped heads. He was clearly uncomfortable and fumbled with the bag, trying desperately to get away from me as quickly as possible.

"Sorry. My fault. Didn't see you." He started to pick up an apple that had rolled away but stopped, hesitant to touch it.

I reached for it and said, "That's okay. I wasn't watching where I was going."

“I can run into the store and get you a new bag. That one’s torn. It’s no trouble. I work there, in the back.”

“Don’t bother. This one’s fine.” I smiled at him which made him even more uncomfortable.

Trying to fill up the silence I said, “Are you new? Don’t think I’ve ever seen you in the store before.”

“Been working here since I came home. Was a cook in the navy.”

We both stood there, too close for him but not for me. I was immediately drawn to him. He reminded me of Elijah.

Even though I knew it was wrong on so many levels, I found myself going out of my way to catch a glimpse of Ernest, looking for him at the market, parking around the back, trying to discover the times he took his breaks.

One day after making an excuse to go to the store, I pulled up to my usual spot and saw him leaning against some boxes, smoking. When he saw me, he lowered his eyes and took a deep deliberate drag on his cigarette.

When our eyes met again, my heart started to race, whether from attraction or guilt I couldn’t tell.

I gave him a brief smile as I got out of the car and walked over to him, keeping what I thought was a respectable distance between us.

“Well, hello again.”

He nodded his head to acknowledge me but said nothing. I took a step closer and trying to keep a light tone said, “We must stop meeting like this.” I could tell my words made him nervous.

“Lady, what do you want?” He threw his cigarette down and crushed it under his shoe.

“Want? I’m just trying to be friendly is all.”

“Friendly, huh. You’d be the first one.” He crossed his arms across his chest and leaned back against the wall. “I’ve seen you, you know, coming in, parking your car here." He glanced around again and took a step closer. His eyes searched mine. "Seems to me you're looking for something more than just friendship."

I was certain he knew the words repeating in my head, heard my heart beating. I took a step closer and softly said, "Maybe I am. Just maybe I am."

Exciting as it was for me, my affair with Ernest didn't last long. He said it wasn't worth the risk, said I didn't understand, would never understand. Perhaps I never would; perhaps I never did.

It wasn't long before I started making excuses to go out at night once the children were in bed, telling Frank I had met a woman who needed a friend, and I wanted to help her out. He said that was a fine thing for me to do. He might have been suspicious knowing I was never one to go out of my way for others, but he stayed silent, something the men in my life had always been good at.

During the next year, I had three brief affairs. As caustic as I knew these "relationships" to be, I sought them out, hoping to still the strange mania that lurked just beneath the surface of my thinking.

That first morning I threw up I knew—knew I had made a terrible mistake, knew I had changed our lives forever, knew I didn't care. I was like the world, once again spinning towards war and unrest, learning nothing from the past, reckless with the future.

Frank looked a little confused when I told him but managed to say, "Helen, that's great. I know you're already overwhelmed, but we can do this…together."

Could we?

He came over to me and gave me a brief hug. I was strangely shocked and annoyed he accepted the news so gracefully. Was he so naïve that he really believed this child was his? The past year, we had been slowly reeling off a cliff, him enjoying the scenery and me screaming all the way down. Now all I felt was the final pull of the already loose thread that was my life.

Edith

1943

Two years have passed since I left home, a mutual decision between my father and me, giving me purpose, he said, tending to my grandfather's aging sister. The ache I carried had stilled my emotions into a listless existence, something my father could not abide. I understand now it was his only recourse to send me away, send me to a place where the daily challenge of my apathy could be hidden from my sister and prying neighbors. It was my unspoken hope this move would eventually quiet the scream that was always just below the surface and bury it beneath the shelter of the pines, in a cabin, beside the lake.

It's been an adjustment for us both. My aunt learning to share her space and me to share myself. Because of our contrary dispositions, there were times of impasse that stretched and challenged.

I found it difficult to understand Elizabeth's contentment in the most mundane tasks, such as stitching a tear in my skirt or kneading bread. I often watched her sitting with eyes closed, holding her worn Bible against her chest, at peace. Even though I tried to put aside my melancholy for her sake, she graciously let me know I was accepted without judgment or distrust. Because I refused any contact with my father and sister, something Elizabeth disagreed with but also accepted, she became my only mirror.

My days were predictable, spent tending her garden, feeding her chickens and two goats and learning to make the cheese she still sold. She taught me to use her old Underwood typewriter, saying I needed to "develop skills." She even tried to teach me how to drive her car, something I detested. I preferred walking to giving control of my destiny over to a machine.

My aunt had gotten even frailer with time, almost completely losing her eyesight. One of my tasks now included reading the Bible to her in the evenings, something that made me uneasy.

"Read that verse to me again will you please? It's my favorite. Oh, yes, I know it by heart, but I love to hear the words spoken to me."

I squirmed in my seat and read Matthew 11:28: "Come unto me, all ye that labor and are heavy laden, and I will give you rest."

"Rest. Do you know that word *rest* not only means to cease your goings-on but to do so you can convalesce and collect your strength. There's a reason to rest." She closed her eyes and sighed.

The silence felt accusatory so I said, "It's getting late, Aunt Elizabeth." I closed her Bible and set it on the table. "I feel a slight chill in the air. I'm going to bring in some more firewood. Mr. Mason dropped off a cord yesterday. Even stacked it nice and neat the way you like. Don't want you getting sick now."

Even though people came and went, I managed to stay apart from the life that swirled around the little cabin. When I suggested she begin to limit her company, a suggestion made more for me than her, she made it clear that anyone who needed friendship and faith were welcome. I never admitted to my aunt how her selflessness shamed me, another reminder of my many flaws. Outwardly sheltered from the turmoil in the world, I was inwardly fighting my own war, a battle lost many times over.

Elizabeth eventually sold the chickens and the goats to one of our neighbors, wanting to lighten my load. She finally agreed to sell the car after I told her I would never drive that "infernal contraption" again after I ran off the road last winter.

A few days before she died Elizabeth called me over and handed me a small piece of notepaper she took from her Bible. I looked at it unable to discern its meaning.

"Edith, here is the name of a reputable family who you might find employment with. I've known them for years, met the daughter when I was just a girl. I..."

"Aunt Elizabeth, do—do you want me to leave? Are you not happy with me? I've tried to be helpful. I know I can be difficult sometimes, but..."

Elizabeth gently patted my hand. "No, no dear." She smiled as she said, "It's just I'm getting older, you know. Lived a good, full life." She fell silent, the only sound the creaking of her rocker and the occasional popping of the fire. "Can't shake this tiredness, though." She started to rub her arm. "My time is coming when I'll go on to Jesus..."

I abruptly interrupted her. "You're fine, Auntie." The mention of her moving on to Jesus brought me back to the memory of Flora telling me that my brother had gone on to Jesus after he was born. "You've just taken a cold, that's all. Here let me get you some tea and stoke the fire." The wind outside started to pick up, brushing branches against the window. I got up, uncomfortable and unnerved.

As I lifted the kettle, I turned. "Aunt Elizabeth, please stay."

I stayed as long as I could. I sat holding the letter my aunt gave me on her death bed, held it like a firm handshake, not wanting to let go. I stopped reading after the first page, unable to continue. Her words sliced me open, the past coming up like bile. Every nerve exposed—*I* was exposed, and I needed to leave.

Two weeks after she died, there was a knock at the door. Mr. Hankins, who owned the local grocery store, stood with hat in hand.

"Excuse me, Miss Edith. I don't mean to disturb you during this difficult time."

"You're not disturbing me. Please come in." Mr. Hankins was a slight man I had known for years. His wife was what you would call a jolly woman, whose smile welcomed all to their thriving market. For some reason, her love of life and her affection for her many children made me feel self-conscious of my reserve. I motioned for him to have a seat.

He fingered his hat nervously. "Miss Edith, before your aunt passed she asked my wife and me if we knew of any positions you might be suited for. I have an acquaintance who manages a beautiful resort down state. He's always looking for honorable help, domestic help. Miss Crandell thought it would be a nice change of scene for you. Get around other young people. The wage isn't much but the position includes room and board."

I grimaced at the thought that I had been a subject of conversation between them but because I knew Elizabeth's intentions were pure, I nodded at his suggestion.

Looking around the cabin, I briefly relived the memories—soft words spoken, selfless actions observed. The realization that my life would never be hers came swiftly.

"Mr. Hankins, I do believe I will take that position. The cabin now belongs to my father, so he will decide what to do with it. It's time I moved on." The finality of those words threatened to betray my forced composure.

"Glad to hear it, Miss. Your aunt would be pleased. I'll make the contacts if that's all right with you."

I nodded my consent.

As he turned to go he added, "She always said God provides and it seems He has."

I stood abruptly, soldier-straight, and said, "Thank you for coming."

That last day, I had one of my neighbor's sons board up the windows, giving him the twenty dollars Elizabeth left me. He had generously offered to take me to the train, one last act of consideration, he said, in honor of a lady who had shown him nothing but kindness. As he picked up my suitcase, he noticed a small wooden box still sitting on the floor by the door.

"Miss Edith, do you want me to put that one in the car?"

I looked over at the box that held the small bird Elijah had carved and Elizabeth's Bible and letter, uncertain as to whether I wanted to carry the hurtful past with me or leave it behind. I softly said, "Yes. Bring that too. Please." As I shut the door for a final time, I stood unable to move.

After a few minutes, he said, "Miss Edith? You'll miss the train if we…"

"I'm coming." I got into the car, slammed the door and never looked back.

I took a position at the stately hotel nestled serenely beside a large lake. Originally a small establishment, it had been rebuilt in 1937 into a stately resort. I was immediately out of place. Serving was beneath me but offered a meager sense of purpose, all I wanted at the time, all I felt I deserved.

I resisted the company of the other servers, unable to join in with their often cruel banter. Ill-mannered words spoken behind backs, ignorant insults against any who did not look or sound as they did annoyed me into a silent aloofness. I was looked down upon, someone to be avoided, which was just fine with me.

As the seasons came and went, the world spun around me—both of us on the edge, still reeling, still uncertain of our futures. From signals bouncing off the moon to earthquakes and giant waves decimating an already ravaged land, the first months of 1946 palpitated between hopeful possibility and random tragedy. I spun with the world between the two.

One morning, as I was setting a table for breakfast, one of the patrons approached me.

"Excuse, me. Miss?"

Slightly startled I respectfully said, "Yes. Can I help you with something?"

I had noticed him before. Mr. Michael Denison was an older gentleman whose younger wife, according to the kitchen gossip, had either recently passed or left him for another man. I had seen them together a few times last summer, quietly taking dinner, leaning in for intimate conversations. She was a slender woman with smooth, auburn hair neatly styled into a Victory Roll. She had a somewhat arrogant demeanor, an air of superiority that kept all but her husband at bay. Perhaps it was just a hesitant sense of where she truly belonged.

His graying hair told me he was probably around my father's age. He was always proper in his dealings with the staff so when he approached me, I was confused at his seeming familiarity.

"Miss…uh"

"Edith is fine. What can I help you with?" I had avoided using my last name whenever possible. I never knew who might be acquainted with my father and didn't want to involve him in my life or my choices.

"Your employer has spoken quite highly of you and your work here."

I was offended being discussed without my consent. "You've been enquiring about me?"

He must have sensed my discomfort and said, "Please don't misunderstand. I have known the man who owns this establishment for many years. We're quite close, you know. When I told him I was in need of a respectable secretary to become a member of my staff, he mentioned you."

"But, sir, I've never been a secretary and here I'm nothing more than a servant."

He gave a brief smile and said, "You don't do yourself justice, Miss Edith. He spoke of your exemplary service and your attention to detail—two extremely important aspects of business."

"Mr. Denison, I am very well situated here, comfortable with my lot. I've no desire to make any changes at this point in my life."

He motioned for me to sit. He pulled up a chair and sat a little too close for my comfort. He leaned in and said, "Edith, my wife…my wife was not only my love and my confidant, she handled aspects of my business that I am finding somewhat tedious. I don't enjoy writing letters or handling the day to day work necessary for my business to continue to be successful. I need someone I can trust, someone who has an attention for detail. I think you are that person."

When I started to object, he stopped me and said, "I have a very large home near Albany. I currently have a live-in staff of three—a housekeeper, a gardener, and a cook. Your wage would be more than you earn as a domestic; we can discuss the details once you have agreed to accept the position. Room and board would, of course, be provided for you. I need an answer by tomorrow as I am leaving at noon. I know this is all very sudden but the needs of my business cannot wait." He stood and offered me his hand as I rose. "Please consider this very respectable offer."

One week later, I was once again packing up my meager belongings to start over. As I got into the car Mr. Denison had sent, some members of the staff gathered to see me off. A few of them wished me well. Some made crude remarks insinuating that I would now be "servicing" Mr. Denison. I lifted my chin and turned away not wanting them to see that their remarks caused me to question my decision.

My room was a small but adequate space on the third floor of a beautiful old, red brick Victorian gracefully situated on five acres at the edge of town. The concerns I had over the respectability of my new employer's offer were quickly alleviated. Mr. Denison was always professional, courteous and appropriate in his dealings with others and with me. As I began to lower my defenses, something I hadn't done in a very long time, I gave myself permission to be happy, with this job and with this fascinating man.

One day, six months after I arrived, we were sitting in his office, me at my typewriter and he at his desk. He had just gotten off the telephone when he said, "Edith, there are some things I'd like to discuss with you."

I grew nervous thinking I had done something wrong and was going to be reprimanded.

He saw the look on my face and said, "Now, don't be concerned. I'm not going to scold you. In fact, you're doing a splendid job. I am very pleased. Here, please sit over here."

He pulled a chair next to his and motioned for me to take a seat. He opened the top drawer of the desk and took out a small pile of letters He sorted through them and handed me a few. "I wanted to show you these."

I carefully took them and noticed they were written in a strange language I had never seen before. "Mr. Denison, I'm not sure what these are. Do you want me to…"

He smiled. "Don't worry. I don't expect you to know what they say." He ran his fingers over the pages. "They are, in fact, just some old letters my parents carried with them when they came to this country." He could see my confusion and added, "They came from Russia in 1890, right through Ellis Island. I was born here, three years later. We lived on the Lower East Side of Manhattan for a while, crammed into a tenement with others seeking a better life, although better is a strong word for life back then." He gave a brief, sad laugh.

"My father was a garment worker for a few years, a very smart man, my father was. Did what he needed to do, learned English, insisted we speak the language of his new country, even at home. Oh, he was proud of his Russian heritage but quickly understood what he would have to do to succeed here." He got up and walked over to the window that overlooked the gardens. Keeping his eyes fixed on the view he said, "His hard work eventually paid off and within eight years he had become a very successful businessman, respected by everyone who knew him."

He came back to where I was sitting and reached for the letters. "That was all, Edith. We can get back to business." I was puzzled by his candor but asked no questions. As I returned to my desk, he stopped me. He extended his hand and said, "Wait. It's only fitting to properly introduce myself. My name is Mika Denisov, and I'm very pleased to make your acquaintance."

The name sounded beautiful as it rolled off his tongue.

We began spending more time together than the members of the household thought proper. Unlike all the others in my life he thought my reticence a positive quality, not being an emotional female. Before the year was over, I became his personal companion, travelled with him, and yes, saw to his needs.

I had never known a man like him, quick-witted in business affairs but compassionate in affairs of the heart. For the next ten years, while the world began and ended a war then began another, Mika and I found refuge in daily walks in the garden and intimate conversations. We were insulated, kept distant from increasing national paranoia. Mika even believed it best he become a very silent partner in his business dealings, not wanting to draw attention to his Russian heritage. It was a sad denial, he said, but a necessary one.

When he passed in 1956, I was left with not only another loss but with a decision to make—where to go next and what to do with my life. I was only thirty-three but felt old, worn. Because we had never married, those who knew of our living arrangements considered me beneath them, tainted. If they only knew.

Mika made sure I would be taken care of and left me fifteen thousand dollars, much to the chagrin of his business partners. I decided to return to where I last knew my sister to be and purchased a small home. I couldn't say why I felt pulled back, felt the need to reconnect. I told myself it was time to go, time to try and make amends. What that actually meant I couldn't say but being alone wasn't good for me. I wanted to continue being the woman Mika believed I was, not the one I knew myself to be.

I hadn't been in my home more than a year when I opened the newspaper and read about an incident involving a woman accused of passing bad checks. It was Helen.

Waiting,
a Pot
Boiling

Genevieve (Eve)

1949-

Was there any story worth my time to tell? I had never been a spectacular woman and accomplished little when I compared myself to others, which I repeatedly did with regret.

What was *my* story? I spent my days reading about fierce women who raised their skirts with abandon to run through dense unplowed fields littered with boundary stones and hope—rows of possibility ploughed deep with sweat and determination. One eye on the horizon and one on tomorrow, they ran after those who had strayed too close to the edge of raging rivers and dangerous decisions.

But what did I run after?

I watched the slow progress of my days, a figure blocked, shoulders silent and bent, whispering out a tattered sigh, a raw breathing in and out of life, myopic, too small and easy to make a lasting impression.

My family? A disastrous swirl of dysfunction. My parents, Helen and Frank, were products of a notion, where Tupperware and Minute Rice signaled their arrival into Middle America. They married in 1946, hopeful that commitment would erase the confusion and stifle the wanderlust that percolated just beneath the surface.

I remembered my father fondly, a man who although scarred and emotionally wounded from the war and my mother's mania, managed to parent us all through her frequent lapses. When he died, he left a void that drained us and fed the legacy of accumulated female guilt that would haunt us all forever.

I found an old photo yesterday, cheap with yellow plastic pressing out the air, closing in two black and white strangers.

My father stood slightly apart from my mother. His hands, clasped together as if in a desperate prayer, pressed against the hairless chest that accommodated his artist's heart, hands that would one day shake crooked under the thought of color.

Even early on I knew my mother was a pistol, cocked, held at the temples of women like Donna Reed in an apron. Gin rummy and canasta, our surrogate Uncle Wiggly. She wrote but never sent stories to *True Romance*, a magazine that early on shaped our view of men. Whether hero or derelict, none satisfied our intense father-longing. For most of my mother's life the rhetorical aphorism of her belief that the universe had set its sights against her hung like a dark cloud over her life, a death sentence in which we were all imprisoned.

After my father's death, there were four of us, then just three, living with a ghost we couldn't seem to send into the light. We surrounded each other like barbed wire on top of a prison fence, keeping us in and others out.

Mary Agnes was the oldest. She was woman who had waited her whole life to grow into her name. Mary once admitted to me her desire for resolution, which went contrary to everything we were as a family, had caused her to wander. When I asked her why she just said, "Why not?"

Frank Jr. and I were born twenty months into Mary's life, conceived out of the frustration of my parent's sleepless nights. For me, there was this space created two minutes after me that had forever changed the way I saw myself, comforted in the womb by each other's arms, a constant presence ripped away by a fateful decision and a tragic accident. I was now one half of a whole. Even now, I seemed to be always seeking the missing part of me, a fleeting image just out of sight who wandered in the peripheral like a floater that blurred my vision.

Frankie and I were six when our father died, signaling for him the need to step into shoes we all knew he couldn't fill. Even at that young age he understood his role, becoming a stable male presence in a turbulent sea of females. When he died, the void scarred us, only worsening with time. Blame and guilt fueled our days, tearing open a rift that ultimately left us aimless and ruined.

I was named after my father's sister, Genevieve—a concession on my mother's part that irked her every time she was forced to use it. Aunt Genevieve was a saintly woman who my mother repeatedly pushed away, more than once ridiculing her keen faith and scorning her attempts at passing it on to us children. My father, who rarely took the lead in our house, insisted on allowing her to take us to church.

The week after he died, I overheard my mother tell my aunt, "No, they're *my* children, not yours. *I* will decide where they go and what they believe. Not you. *No*! We don't need the interference of you *or* your God. Just leave us alone!" The slam of the receiver almost took the phone off the wall and dashed my young hope of heaven and seeing my father again.

Alice was the last. Only three and a half when she came along, Frank and I were old enough to sense that her arrival upset our family's already fragile equilibrium. There were bitter words muffled from behind closed doors and my mother's often biting remarks deepened our love and compassion for Alice.

Two months before my father clutched his chest and never woke up Frankie chased Alice around his chair with a crayon saying he was going to "connect the dots" on her freckled face. My father snatched Alice up as she flew by, took her in his arms and lovingly wiped away her tears.

"You mustn't hurt your sister's feelings, Frank. I know you really didn't mean to hurt her. Now say you're sorry."

Frank lowered his head. "I'm sorry, Alice."

"Mary, Eve, come here." We all gathered around my father. "Children, words can hurt just like you were hit by a stone, just as painful. You know how sometimes it's hard to understand Nonna and Pop, especially when they get excited?" We all giggled because we knew what our father meant. "Now you would never make fun of them…"

Our voices joined, "Never, Papa."

My father smiled. "That's right. You see, they have an accent that has set them apart. Did you know when they first came to this country from Italy people were often cruel, refusing them jobs and even where they could live, just because they were…different?"

The thought that others didn't love our Nonna and Pop like we did caused us all to rally around Alice. My father, despite his shortcomings, made it clear we were greatly loved by him and by a God who we were all still uncertain of. My mother, on the other hand, only mentioned God when it was followed by a *dammit*.

When my father died, my mother's past and present indiscretions were heaped on us all, especially Alice. One night a woman named Mrs. O'Neil came to our door and accused my mother of having an affair with her husband. Even though we didn't fully understand we knew how dangerous the threat of anger could be.

After that night, words, slurs really, followed us all, even at school. Frankie began fighting with the other boys, while Mary tried her best to mother us, a hollow comfort but a comfort nevertheless. I began to turn my fear in on myself, stuffing my confusion down with my food. Something I do to this day.

The only other woman who circled us was my mother's sister, Edith. She and my mother had reconciled a year after my father died, if reconcile meant tolerate. She discovered her older sister had been living not ten miles from us. We never really understood what caused the strain between them but knew to stay clear of asking.

We moved in with her two years later, right after a rock came crashing through our living room window one night. There was a note attached to it, which my mother quickly tore up. All I know is that she looked at us and said, “Pack what you can. We’re leaving within the hour.” The look on her face scared us. We had seen the hard lines and clenched jaw before but this time the seething anger that rose up from her became a looming presence in the room. We just looked at each other and did as we were told not wanting to add fuel to my mother’s simmering rage, uncertain of the consequence if we did.

Edith was a woman who, to us, lived a distant half-life. She tolerated us like the unfortunate offspring of my mother’s sins, all except for Alice who for some reason could do no wrong. Grateful as we were to be away from the violence of my mother’s poor choices in men, our lives were lived blanketed by our aunt’s imposing presence and the banal brown and Halloween-orange knitted wraps that flew from her fitful fingers. The Morse-code ticking of metal knitting needles was the background music to our days as they bit through the air like one of her cold remarks.

I remembered how her Scarlett O’Hara lips pressed unfiltered Camels, lit one to another, a smokescreen few dared to penetrate. We spent years watching her as she rolled her petulance into rum balls shaped between the choler and the calluses. They would roll around the creases of her lifeline, pushing out and forced to move along. One hundred proof molasses kept her hands warm and almost clapping, close enough to control the rounding-rhythm of each damp cake, but just far enough apart to stifle the sound. Moist shots, powdered into confection, distilled in antique tins—sublimation at its best.

Our lives were colorless under her critical eye as one by one we waited to break away from the bondage of her flinty gloom. A hard anger with an unknown history, lingered beneath the surface of my mother and her sister.

Waiting, a pot boiling, whose lid was ready to blow.

Mary Agnes

1947-

I had always seen myself in relation to others—a father's first obedient daughter, a sibling's first mother-figure, a mother's first frustration. I don't remember much before the twins were born, just hazy glimpses of dissatisfaction and harsh words from my mother.

Memories, some good yet brief with meaning, came and went…sand between my toes, the smell of pine, the sound of water lapping, the distant laughter of my father and grandfather, sisters and brother. They warmed whenever they intruded into what my life had become.

Ever since I was nine, I've thought my name begged an air of spiritual propriety. Mary Agnes, Sister Mary Agnes, pious and committed, a life of selfless service and faith.

I attended my first Catholic service with a friend and her mother when I began my fascination with the prospects of respectability. I spent the weekend at her house, and it was expected I accompany them to church that Sunday morning. The only other church I had been in was a small unassuming clapboard with worn seats with a dusty woodstove in the back. But this…this was unlike anything I had ever seen—dark, polished wood, glass windows stained with the images of deliverance and death, the slight smell of incense, the imposing stance of marbled saints stationary in their devotion, the ceremony of repentance that was confirmed on velvet-covered kneelers. Men in robes, their strange words echoing their meaning against the vaulted ceiling, drew me in to the ceremony and the mystery.

I noticed a few women clothed with the signs of their faith, penitently silent and bowed into hands clasped tight before them. When I got home, I imagined my life as one of those women, cloistered and unassuming. That afternoon I built a small altar out of an old dresser with a shoebox on top that housed a small pocket-sized Bible my aunt had given me and a few plastic statues discretely gleaned from my friend's bedroom. When no one was around, I would take out my shoebox, kneel before the dresser, hands clasped tight like the women, praying to a God I wasn't sure heard me.

I finally graduated college in '68, a dismal affair, with a degree in whatever, which did nothing to prepare me for what my life became…whatever. I married Richard on a cold March day two years later because I wanted to get away from my mother and all her drama and honestly, I had nothing else to do at the time.

I met my husband shortly after Alice ran away to marry some flighty musician. Who was I to blame her for her poor choices? We had all scattered, fled like rats from a sinking ship. We were a fractured lot, Eve, Alice and me, women on the edge with no place to go but down.

In the beginning, I thought Richard smart and witty. Looking back, I realize his only interesting quality was the unique way he could organize his underwear drawer so that the tops of his socks were intimately tucked into the legs of his boxers like some bizarre underwear mating ritual.

Our brief union produced one son, Rickie, who couldn't wait to flee my manic mothering style that swung between…how did he put it? Between the "Grand Canyon and a tomb." I told him he was clever for a ten-year-old, and I retreated to my place in the canyon. It was the final birth push that sent him half-way across the country to live with his father later that year. A decision we all agreed was best. The day after he turned twenty-seven, he married. His father sent me the newspaper announcement after the fact, a paper knife that hit its mark.

In spite of my desire to move on, my life was destined to a slow progress made even slower by the questionable choices I made after my son left.

Throughout the years of attempting to make Richard feel like more, I had become less, despising everything about myself, all 5'11 inches of me, not just because my height made Richard feel short and insignificant, but because it seemed to give men, particularly short men, permission to talk to my chest.

Because my life had become narrow by years of self-doubt, the week after Rickie left to live with his father I took an unassuming office job at the local college. Surrounded by those who were on their way to becoming…more, I was content to keep my head down and put one foot in front of the other. That is until I met Oliver.

Alice

1952-2019

I was born at odds with myself. Accepted but kept at a distance by unspoken words and strained looks, I tried to blend in and cover up the many freckles that were a permanent reminder that my face was set apart, marked by a fate I didn't understand. I even pulled my barn-red, unruly hair into braids so tight my head hurt. But whatever I did I was still…different.

Except for the expected conflicts, my sisters and brother tolerated me, treated me as the annoying little sister that I was. My father, although reticent in nature, was affectionate with us all, trying his best to make up for my mother's more remote parenting style. When he died, he left a hole that to this day has never been filled.

When I was five, two years after my father died, I overheard my mother talking with one of our neighbors, a woman whose interest in our affairs was as obvious as her perfectly manicured lawn. She commented on how, oh how did she put it? How "curious" it was that my features were so different from my siblings. My mother forced a laugh and said, "Oh, she takes after my husband's father."

She abruptly shuffled me into the car and slammed the door. Her look of shame, a mixture of pain and disgust, had stayed with me, coloring the way I saw myself for years.

What was left of our family slid silently back into Edith's life after the accident we never talked about, without acknowledgement or debate. We were all wounded, physically and emotionally, falling headfirst into the space none of us could fill.

One year to the day we were off again, this time without harsh words or anger. The week before I had overheard my mother tell my aunt that if she "wanted the cabin she'd have to pay for it."

When Edith left for work, my mother gathered us up in her usual manic fashion. Since there was no fight the only thing left to do was flight. What my mother deemed better for her was never what was best for me. So the day after I turned ten, my mother moved us in with her current love interest—a man who oddly resembled my father. The good thing was that they kept to themselves. Marcus drove a truck, and my mother got a job at the local lounge as a waitress.

Mary was fifteen, a few years from graduating, and Eve, now thirteen, held her breath and kept her head down, finding comfort in food and becoming a singular shadow without Frankie.

By the time I was fourteen, I stayed away as much as I could, spending time with my only two friends. I found an acceptance with Mira and Carlos that I didn't feel at home. We shared this peculiar connection, bonded together by the sting of a narrow-minded world.

Even though Mira's father was white, her Japanese mother was the object of malicious remarks from those who refused to forget the horrors of Pearl Harbor. I thought her beautiful, mysterious-looking. She was shy around others but with us, sheltered in our friend's basement, she sang, danced, smoked and laughed. Carlos, well Carlos, had a darker complexion and still carried the accent that singled him out. Whenever someone made fun of the way he spoke, he laughed and cursed at them in Spanish.

Everything changed when in 1968 Carlos' older brother, Donato, returned home after a one year spree in California and introduced us to Joplin, Hendrix, and Santana. We loved their flaunting of convention and even the raw vocals of Bob Dylan and other misfits who proudly leaned into their differences and thrived, something we all secretly wished we could do. He also introduced us to weed.

Of course, my mother didn't approve, not in my choice of friends, not of my choice in music, not in my awakening to a world that was simultaneously pulling me in and drowning me. I stayed distant from my sisters, a way of protecting myself from their caring albeit snide remarks about my life. I had learned well to hide beneath the mud of innuendo and suffocate my desire without notice.

When I was sixteen, I got a part-time job at a small book store in town where I was surrounded by words that stirred and carried me, fed me. Mr. Jenkins owned the small shop, a man who once admitted to me he was living a double life. I appreciated his honesty but as one who understood the need for secrets, I passed no judgement and asked no questions.

It was 1969, a year before I was to graduate high school, that he took me aside and gave me a book of poems.

"Alice, I've watched you this past year, seen you scribbling in that notebook of yours, recording, thinking. Hard worker, considering where you came from." He knew most in town which made him privy to all the gossip about my mother. He was never one to mince his words around me. "Consider it an early graduation present."

I shyly thanked him and tucked it in my backpack.

I was overwhelmed when I began to flip through the pages. Here was a black woman, another Alice, with a strong voice who had the courage to say whatever she wanted. I was caught even before I started reading her poems with the blurb in the beginning by someone named Albert Camus: "To correct a natural indifference I was placed half-way between misery and the sun. Misery kept me from believing that all was well under the sun, and the sun taught me that history wasn't everything." *History wasn't everything.*

1970-1971

My senior year began with yet another move. My mother had grown tired of Marcus and discarded him like the old clothes she said no longer fit. Because Mary and Eve were both married and kept to themselves, a decision I resented but understood, I was alone now with a mother who was barely there even when she was physically present and her shady boyfriend, a man who spent more time looking at me than at my mother.

The conflict that ate away at me was not just my mother's doing. War, scandal, discrimination, the soundtrack of my senior year, pounded its jarring rhythm into everything. The madness threatened to devour me. My slow descent came full circle when instead of going to prom I drank and smoked myself into nothingness, at least for a few hours.

I was still drunk.

I woke up on my back, soaked through, but didn't care. I stared up at the night sky and tried to focus. My heart began to pound out, a derelict sob that threatened to come to the surface. The moon peered out from passing clouds and made me feel watched, judged.

Dumped like an old can, I just laid there discarded on the cold side of a disinterested fence noticed only by some random dog. He accosted the wire hedge between us like a rabid baby throwing a tantrum, broadcasting my indiscretion.

I turned and whispered as if I was in church. "Do you have a light?" His damp hand brushed my cheek just a little too casual.

The park was empty. Contentious weeds forced my fingers apart and pushed into the hard ground of my open palms. I glanced over at the sleeping form beside me.

What was it about him?

The air, imposing and edgeless, pressed against my body, uninvited. Like a medium, I took a deep drag of my cigarette and coughed out a ghostly annulet and blew it at his back, making him look like a Cimmerian specter, just passing through.

What was it about his words, his heat? I held my hands over my swollen eyes then felt a rush.

Maybe it was the way he penetrated my staleness, coursed through my void, crawled over my inhibitions like fences.

But this time there were no kisses. This time the past was not a diminishing emptiness like before. This time the night exploded with poisonous sighs that seemed to lie everywhere, just taking up space—a lot like zero.

I took another drag and flopped back onto the wet grass, chilled more from my choices than the early morning air. I shivered. I had done it again. Gotten wasted with Donato, a man I promised Carlos I'd never see again.

Why did I do this?

I sat back up and hugged my knees, held them like a breath.

I feel helpless like I'm caught inside the spin of some random tornadic twist of fate that winds me back around and around like a sheet whipped in the wind, shaken dry by sheer force.

I laughed at my witty appraisal and flicked the cigarette away. *Yeah, just like me to fictionalize my stupidity.*

Rolling away I eventually stood, weak and dizzy. I rubbed my face again and tried to bring myself back.

My days are full of wicked witches on brooms, frantic dogs barking from baskets. Going home will take more than a few simple clicks. Oz is a dream, and I cannot fall asleep.

I said aloud to no one in particular, "Not bad." I left Don face-down in the grass, snoring into the ground, indifferent to my leaving. I walked out of the deserted park and down the still-dark streets toward home glad there was only a stray cat to observe my shame.

I never thought I'd get caught. That's what they all say, isn't it? It was only a couple of joints after all. But even when I walked toward his suspicious hair lying too perfect across his too perfect face I knew it was wrong. But my conscience was held fast in that rebel thrill, and I couldn't stop. Not even when that sick sense twisted inside again. Not even when I saw an old friend of my mother's crossing the street. Not even when that stupid Jesus freak tried to hand me something. Not even…I was never going to stop. Neglect had worn through me nearly as much as my random thoughts and ground me into the dust. *I am dust.*

"Time to go." The officer clanged open the bars. "Let's go!" When I looked confused, he snidely said, "Guess your mother has *friends* in high places." His suggestive laugh shamed me more than a night in jail but not as much as knowing I had been arrested for a thrill and not for standing against injustice.

Once released, things at home remained somewhat the same. As usual, my mother never spoke of how she got me released and just ignored what she called my "slight lapse in judgment," while her new boyfriend was intrigued I was open to crossing a line. The only evidence I had been arrested was my random scribbling in my journal:

This still, hot night-suspended—I watch these elastic shadows dance before my bloodshot eyes; they snap tight around my pallid skin, embrace me through to a place where black meets black and agrees. Here in this swollen, concrete box, I sit; knees caught up captive, held like a breath just long enough to get a rush. My shoulder, bent like flamed wax, becomes home to an old woman's delusion. I shake her loose and feel the greasy imprint of her burden on my clothes. I hide my regret like booty and pretend that I am dangerous, but really, I am only cold; cold past my damaged heart, beneath my fragile frame, cold like hell. I am just like you, old woman—bobbing back at the last moment, jerking against invisible arms, searching for a shoulder to hold my burden for even just one night. We are the same need.

Donato was also pulled to my flirt with the illegal and started to come around more. At first, I was glad for the diversion of his attention but soon the drama that surrounded him became its own kind of prison. Every night the crisis he craved increased, knocking at my door like some God-forsaken opportunity, waiting to shock my attention into action. He said we were good for each other because we understood the crazy that haunted us both.

I married him four months after high school, a mistake we both acknowledged an hour after we stood before a justice of the peace. Donato was everything I didn't want in a man. He believed the three days he spent partying with Mira at Yasqur's farm set him apart, bragging to whoever would listen that it made him an exceptional musician in tune, he said, with our generation's pulse for change. But Don wasn't really big on change. Playing his guitar and singing in dismal bars at night, he'd sleep off the previous night's drugged haze—his revolution.

I'd numb myself when I could, just enough to stand my miserable life. My job at the bookstore was my only relief but ended abruptly the day after Mr. Jenkins came into work and told me he was selling the shop, said he just couldn't afford to keep it open anymore. No cutomers. When I asked him why people stopped coming in he just put his hand on my shoulder and shook his head. I knew he had become more critical over the years, speaking out against the discrimination and bigotry he believed was destroying the country. I just never knew the cost.

I'll never forget the defeat I saw in his eyes, a cultural sadness hung around his shoulders. He went over to the door and turned the open sign over. I was overcome with anger and said, "They can't make you go away."

He turned to me and smiled. "I'll never stop working for the dream, dear Alice. But never let your anger turn inward or else they win. And if they win, we all lose."

He sold the shop later that week and moved away, leaving no forwarding address.

Don and I also moved that spring, crashing with some of his friends who rented a loft. I inwardly hated being indebted but as always, I slid into the void without complaint.

1972

"Come on. Hurry up. You're not the only one who needs to get in there." Snickers came from behind the bathroom door. "We can *hear* you." More laughs then a pounding.

"Alice, move it!" The noise had woken up Don who was not happy.

When my sickness became a regular morning occurrence it strangely amused our roommates, a joke about my habits. But I suspected there was another reason.

When I first found out I was pregnant, panic almost swollowed me whole. The constant parties and chaos that swirled around us told me this was no place for a baby, but despite my misgivings I chose life, whether from a sense of decency or, more likely, from a futile sense of whatever.

We named our daughter Carlotta after Don's sister who passed away the year before. I understood him wanting to honor his sister, but I hated his reasoning, naming our daughter after someone who died in her excess, a sad casualty of the times. I knew all too well how a name could shape a destiny. One night after polishing off her last bottle my mother told me I had been named after the character in *Alice in Wonderland* because once you went down the rabbit hole, you just never knew what would happen. Throughout the years, I had descended down that hole and had lived with the mad remnants of my past.

I was a mess, still reeling from years of avoiding life at all costs. Even though I stopped getting high, I found myself being pulled in after my daughter was born, just something to take off the edge of who I was and who I wasn't. Surrounded by friends, not friends really, who lived their lives in a haze, I decided to join them.

Carli was a contented baby, hard to imagine when all around her was chaos. I knew I needed to get it together when I couldn't remember if I changed her. Was it last night? This morning? The flaming red rash told me what I already knew. I was replaying the past, a negligent mother.

I found reasons to remove myself from the constant party that went on in the loft. People came and went, some stayed a few days, some more. I couldn't say anything because we were two of those people who crashed for one night and never left.

I wasn't sure where the money came from but deep down I knew Donato was dealing and doing who knows what to feed us and his habit. That morning when I discovered his body, cold and still, I'm embarrassed to say underneath my grief, I felt a sudden relief. With the last needle push, Donato had unintentionally ended what I could not.

But now what to do, where to go? I reluctantly called Eve but when her husband found out it was me, he took the phone away from her, making it clear I wasn't welcome. Asking Mary was out of the question. So who was left? My mother? Disconnected as usual. Aunt Edith. Could I do it? Call and lay all my failures before her for her to criticize like she did my mother? Once again I sank back down into the hole, chased by the white rabbit of my past.

"Where is that stupid number?" There was no place left to look. I pulled my old backpack out from the back of the closet. *I can't believe I still have this. Don't even remember what's in it.*

What I did remember was the scene it caused. As I shoved whatever I could find into the pack, my mother screamed curses about what an ungrateful daughter I was. I knew moving out to marry Donato was a mistake but to me anything was better than living in the hell that had become my life.

I pulled out a few old notebooks and crumpled papers. Memories came flooding back, making me feel smaller and smaller. "Got it!" Scribbled onto the back of an old postcard was her number. Breathing a sigh of relief I quickly realized I was going back to where I said I'd never go back from a place I thought I'd never be.

Edith

1972

"Aunt Edith, he's dead." The phone rang into the silence that was my nightly companion. With those words I was brought back, reliving the night Helen tore her children from me and sacrificed them to her selfishness.

"Aunt Edith? Are you there?"

"Alice? What's—who's dead?" I had tried to stay in touch with Alice, sporatic letters and phone calls came and went, but the past few years she just disappeared.

Silence. Then…"Don. Donato's dead. I tried to wake him up this morning, but he was gone. I slept out on the couch again with…with." Alice sobbed out her words. "The leather strap…the needle was still in his arm. Some friends tried to help before they took off, afraid of the police, but I knew it was too late. It was always too late. I don't know what to do or where to go." Silence again.

"Alice, where are you?"

"We've been living in a friend's loft, but he moved out a month ago. We were being evicted. I tried to call Mom but her phone was disconnected. Evie's husband made it clear I wasn't welcome, not that I could blame him. Mary…I just can't disappoint her again."

Alice was rambling the words rushing out, a torrent of pain and shame. "Alice, stop. Calm down." *Was I going to regret my next words*?

After the accident, Helen and the girls moved back in with me. I held my tongue the best I could. Yes, I blamed my sister for the death of her son, but if I was honest, I also blamed myself. The bitterness that was such a part of my life had finally pushed her to an end neither of us could see at the time.

"Alice, come stay with me. I know I can be difficult but we've always gotten along. I still live in the same house, you know the one on Mathis Ave. It's not much but the neighbors mind their own business."

Alice stopped crying long enough to say, "I…I have a daughter, Aunt Edith. Her name is Carlotta…Carli I call her, and she's six months old. She's a good baby. Hardly ever cries."

I opened my mouth but the only words that came out were, "A child?"

"Aunt Edith? I know I'm asking a lot but…"

I interrupted, "Where are you? I'll send you bus money. I never got a car. Let me know what the schedule is, and I'll meet you. What's your phone number?"

"I'm using a friend's phone. Ours was cut off months ago. I'll call you as soon as I know anything. And thank you, Aunt Edith. You have no idea how alone I've been."

But I did know.

A

Disjointed

Narrative

Alice

1979

These past seven years with Edith had been a time of growth and trial, growth for me as I learned to feel and deal with, well, deal with life and trial because Edith's crusty demeanor kept me and Carli at a distance. I had no idea what made her this way and more often than not, I didn't care.

Carli, now seven, was growing into everything I never was at her age. Whenever I tried to braid her hair she said she wanted her "crazy hair to fly free in the wind." Her deep brown eyes and darker complexion made her look a bit exotic, a look that reminded me of her father—a look that both saddened and haunted me.

Last month as I fixed her a sandwich, I noticed her staring at me. "Carli, what's the matter?" As I put the bread down, my heart suddenly began to race.

"Mom, where's my daddy?"

Even though I knew this day would come I was ill-prepared to give my daughter an acceptable answer.

I hesitated but knew I needed to continue. "Well, Carli, he died when you were a baby."

She took the words in with the look that suddenly aged her.

"How did he die?"

The gut-punch left me breathless.

"Mom?"

"I heard you, Carli." Even though I had practiced the words for the last year wanting to be prepared when the time came, I didn't expect it so soon. I came around the counter and pulled a chair up next to her. A wave of motherly love washed over me, something I was just beginning to understand.

“Carli, your father was a very…passionate man who felt the things of this world very deeply. The details of his death aren’t for you right now. All you need to know is that if he could see you and the wonderful little girl you are he would do anything to be here with both of us.” I saw her thinking beyond her years.

“Do you have a picture of him?”

“No, I’m sorry I don’t. Maybe if I can find your Uncle Carlos he might have one.” I immediately regretted my words.

“I have an Uncle Carlos?” Her face brightened.

It had been so many years. Once we married, Donato cut all ties with his family. They never approved of me or our lifestyle. When he died, I gave the police all the information I had and left them to sort through disposing of his body. I was unable and unwilling to put to rest a man who lost his life years before he died. The chances were slim I would now be able to track Carlos down, but I wanted to give Carli a weak hope of family.

Edith was right about the neighbors. They mostly kept to themselves, all except for Minerva, her husband, Isaiah, and their sixteen-year-old daughter, Harriet. Their house was directly behind ours with the backyards butting up against each other. Every time I went out, she was there…gardening, hanging her wash or just sitting with eyes closed, face lifted up towards—I don’t know what.

They moved in eight months ago much to the chagrin of the family to the right of us who said they didn’t want people like *them* living in their neighborhood. Said it caused property values to decrease. Personally, I thought it was their obnoxious teenagers who brought the values down.

Oddly enough, Edith had formed a strange affinity for Minerva’s daughter, Harriet, especially since the signs of pregnancy began to show. I had even seen my aunt smile when she saw her, very uncharacteristic for someone who was distant from the rest of the world.

Edith, who was a very private person, was not one to let anyone beneath her hard exterior. I didn't know anything about her life before or after we finally left her in '62, but lately she had become much more moody, more unsettled. Her job as a nurse's aide, which she had for more than twenty years, was coming to an end, and she was retiring. A strange job, I thought, for someone who didn't seem moved by other's pain.

Later that week, after the bus picked Carli up for school, I decided to take a chance and ask. "Aunt Edith, would you mind if I asked you something? It's none of my business, but I was just wondering."

She suddenly got a frantic look, stiffened up and finally said, "What do you want to know?"

"It's about Harriet."

Without a word, Edith went into her bedroom where I thought she'd stay. I stood still, more uncomfortable than I had been in a long time. A few minutes later, Edith appeared at the door and motioned for me to come. I entered the room and saw her sitting on her bed with the small wooden box that was a constant on her dresser.

"Alice, come sit by me, here on the bed."

I walked over and sat on the chenille spread as far away as I could without offending.

"Alice, I've had this box for oh, since I was a young girl." She gave a brief but sad smile and patted its worn top, hesitant to go further.

Feeling even more uncomfortable I said, "Aunt Edith, you don't have to..."

"Yes, I do, Alice. I've needed to do this for a very long time." She opened the lid and pulled out some yellowed letters, a tattered Bible, and a small carved bird. She laid the Bible aside and gently picked up the bird.

"You see this? Someone very special made this for me one Christmas. It was to be the last thing I ever received from him."

The question I was to ask her was one I wasn't sure I wanted to know the answer to. "Who gave you this gift?"

As tears pooled in her eyes, she looked up at me and said, "Elijah gave this to me…just before he was murdered."

The next two hours the pain, heartache, and bitterness poured out of Edith like acid rain, bringing her to the point of exhaustion by the time she was silent. Memories, sharp as the days they were formed, brought her back and left her at the doorstep of her life—loving Eli, giving birth to Esther, leaving her with Mabel, living with her great-aunt, and finally the years spent working for and then loving Michael, Mika. I sat motionless, stunned by her words, shamed by my youthful judgment of her.

"Aunt Edith, I never knew…"

Edith, who had never once looked me in the eyes as she told me her story, now fixed her gaze on me. "It was never yours to know." She hastily put her treasures back in their box, closed the lid, got up and placed them back on her dresser.

I hesitated before asking, "Is that why you smile at Harriet because you know what it's like to be—you know?"

With her back still to me she said, "I think it's time I got dinner ready. I want the soup to simmer." Edith turned and placed her hand on my shoulder. "Carli will be home soon. It's good to meet her at the bus stop."

That was all she said.

Two months after our conversation, I happened to meet Minerva and her daughter at the market. I had seen them a few aisles over but strategically avoided going the same way, not wanting an awkward encounter. As I turned the corner of the aisle, there they were, smiling as if they were waiting for me.

Minerva pulled her cart up next to mine and said, “Alice, isn’t it? Edith’s niece? This is my daughter, Harriet, and as you can see there’s going to be a blessed event in around two months time.”

There was no shame, no embarrassment in her tone. She was genuinely excited she was to be a grandmother. “Harriet, could you please go and get the last few things on the list?”

Harriet shyly said, “Of course, Mom.” She came closer to me and said, “I’m glad we met.” She started to go but stopped. “If you ever need a babysitter I’d be glad to. I’ve seen your daughter in the yard. She looks sweet.”

I thanked her. Minerva watched her daughter leave then looked at me. “I know how some people think it’s shameful what Harriet has done. They look at the life in her and want her to be ashamed and sorrowful over it. Oh, don’t get me wrong. We’ve had the talk about right living and the consequence of wrong, but that’s in the past and this new life, this innocent little life has no part in her shame. And you have to know I will fight like a mother hen anyone who tries to make this less than the blessing that it is.”

I mumbled out, “That’s nice” and excused myself as politely as I could. I was shaken by her words, especially after what I had heard from Edith.

As awkward as our first meeting was I found myself drawn to Minerva’s welcoming demeanor. I began accepting her invitations to visit especially whenever Edith sank into one of her moods. The joy housed within her home was the balm I desperately needed. Carli loved Harriet, liked putting her hand on her belly waiting for the baby to kick it off.

Harriet had begun babysitting whenever I had an evening class. Edith insisted I take a few courses at the local community college, said I needed to acquire skills, advance my learning. Despite being overwhelmed at times, I enjoyed mingling with those who had direction and at least a small vision of what they wanted to become.

Late on a snowy January there was a knock at the door. It was Minerva.

"I'm so sorry to bother you at this late hour but I wanted to share the happy news."

She was beaming as I welcomed her in.

"At 7:45 this evening Harriet gave birth to a healthy baby girl. Both momma and baby are doing well."

"Congratulations, Minerva." I turned to where Edith was cleaning up the kitchen. "Edith, did you hear? Harriet has had her baby." Silence. Slightly embarrassed I repeated myself. "Edith, did you hear me? Harriet…"

From the other room Edith flatly said, "I heard. How wonderful for you both."

I turned to Minerva and weakly smiled. She put her hand on my arm, quietly reassuring me.

Trying to change the direction of the moment, I asked, "Did she choose a name yet?"

"Yes. Had it picked out months ago just in case it was a girl. Named her Esther. Harriet wanted to thank my sister, her favorite aunt, for all of her support during this somewhat difficult time. Her full name is bigger than she is—Esther Ruth Anne. She said she didn't want to leave her other aunts out of the naming. Didn't include my sister, Harriet, for obvious reasons since she carries her name already." Minerva was beaming. "I'll have to bring…"

We heard a plate break on the floor and turned and saw Edith white as a ghost, holding on to the door frame.

"Aunt Edith, what's wrong?"

"What did you say the baby's name was?" She inched forward.

"Why, it's Esther. An old-fashioned name but a strong one."

I could see Edith unravel before my eyes. I looked back at Minerva. Suddenly aware of the possibility.

Edith inched forward. "How old is your sister Esther?"

Somewhat confused, she answered, "Well, she's forty. Two years older than me. Esther was a little different than the rest of us children, but…"

Edith interrupted, "Different how?"

"Well, her hair and skin tone were lighter, but the details surrounding Esther were off limits. Our parents made sure of that. Said it was a private matter belonging only to Esther and to God. It wasn't until many years later that I learned more than my mother would have liked. Why?"

I looked over at Edith. She practically whispered, "Minerva, what was your mother's name?"

"My mother's name? Why it was Mabel, passed just this past March. Shame she won't see her first great-grandchild. She…"

Edith interrupted, "Excuse me. I need to go lie down." She moved passed us like an exorcised spirit, barely there but purposeful in her release.

Minerva came over to me and whispered, "Did I say something wrong? She seems so…distraught."

How could I explain what was reeling inside me without betraying a confidence?

"I really can't say. Why don't we just leave this for now?" I ushered a confused Minerva to the door. "Tell Harriet we'll stop over in a few days. Carli will be thrilled."

Edith stayed behind closed doors for the remainder of the evening. I wanted to tell her it was just some strange coincidence, that the odds of Minerva being the sister of her daughter were beyond…beyond what?

The next morning I gently knocked on her door, "Aunt Edith? I made you some tea and toast. I thought you'd like some…"

"I don't want anything but to be left alone!"

Carli came over to me. "Mom, what's the matter with Aunt Edith? Is she sick?"

"Yes, honey. She's not feeling well. Let's just give her a chance to rest."

In the midst of Edith's slow breakdown and my job and schooling, I received a letter from Carlos.

After searching multiple phone books from surrounding areas, along with towns around where I knew his family had lived, I came across his name, well actually two names. They were both Carlos Rodriguez but different addresses. I sent the same letter to both just saying I was an old friend who wanted to reconnect. Now as I held his letter in my hand, I questioned my decision to open a new rift in the past.

The writing was rushed, almost a frenzied scribble:

Alice,

Weird to hear from you. After Donato died had crazy thoughts about you. Was in the city and found the loft a few weeks later, but a man who was there said he never heard of you or Don.

So much has gone down, not sure where to begin, not sure best said in a stupid letter. Just got back, was in Mexico, trying to get my head on straight. Write me back. Don't have a phone. Maybe we can pick up where we left off.

Carlos

I stared at the words for I don't know how long, feeling—what? *He came to the loft*? *Was in Mexico*?

I didn't share this news with my daughter, not yet. I wanted to be certain before bringing any more drama into our lives. I wrote another brief letter, and against my better judgment, included my phone number. Even though I felt an unnamed dread, I needed to connect to what was behind me before I could move forward.

And now I would wait—wait while surrounded by a ghost from my past and an unknown one from Edith's, wait while an uncertain present unfolded and wait for the conclusion of a formless future. Maybe nothing would come of this anyway.

A week after the letter arrived we visited Minerva and Harriet, at least Carli and I did. The baby was beautiful and Harriet was taking her responsibility as a mother very seriously.

I waited to speak with Minerva about my suspicions until I could wait no longer. A few days later when Edith finally left her room and went to the store and Carli was in school, I stopped by.

"So sorry to bother you again, but I wanted to drop off these muffins I made."

"Come in, come in. Harriet, Alice is here with goodies." Minerva smiled as she took my coat. "So glad you came. I hope Edith and Carli are well."

"Yes, Carli can't wait to come over again. Said she doesn't want Esther to forget her."

"And Edith? Do you think we'll see her anytime soon?"

I intentionally ignored her last question. "Minerva, I wanted to talk with you…"

Just then Harriet came from the other room carrying a laundry basket.

She whispered, "Hello. It's good to see you again. Esther Ruth is asleep, but you can always look in at her."

"Thanks, but I don't want to disturb her. I just stopped by to see your mom and deliver these muffins. How are you doing?"

Harriet put the basket down and began to sort the clothes. "I think I'm getting the hang of this. I'm tired, but Mom says that's natural." She stopped mid-fold and said, "As soon as I can I'm going to finish my schooling, only had a few more months to go anyway. Then I'm going to go to nursing school."

Minerva broke in. "Harriet was so taken by the nurses who took care of her, she decided even before she left the hospital that she wanted to be just like them."

"It'll be hard and all with Esther, but Mom said she'd help out whenever she could. I even heard from Esther's father the other day."

Minerva turned away from her daughter, closed her eyes for a moment and took a deep breath. As if on cue, Esther Ruth let out a big cry from the other room. "Best feed your daughter now, dear."

"Okay, Mom. So glad you stopped by." Harriet moved the basket to behind the couch and went to attend to her daughter.

Minerva put her arm around my shoulder and said, "Let's sit in the kitchen where we can talk.

I watched while Minerva fixed us some coffee, hesitating with each movement. She finally sat down and leaned in.

"Is there something you want to ask me maybe, but you're hesitant? Am I close?"

The fact I couldn't look her in the eyes made it obvious even to me. Slightly embarrassed I said, "Yes. I do have something to ask. I'm not sure how to say this, but I'm very worried about my aunt."

"I see." Minerva got up, took two cups from the cupboard and placed them on the table. She brought the carafe over and began to slowly fill each one. As she pulled out the chair next to me she said, "I've been concerned myself especially since that night when I came over to announce Esther's birth. I've been praying especially hard for her lately. Is she in deep distress over something?"

"That's what I wanted to discuss with you. Without betraying any confidences, I wonder if you could tell me about your sister, Esther."

"Esther? But why?"

I started to tear up, felt myself beginning to dissolve right before Minerva's eyes. I stood and hung on to the back of the chair, hoping that my grip would strengthen my resolve. Finally I just blurted out, "Because I think your sister, Esther, is Edith's daughter!"

Minerva silently took my words in, weighing their meaning. She motioned for me to sit back down. Reaching for my hands, she held them, covered them. "Well now; let's see if we can make sense of all this, see if we are all more than just neighbors."

As Minerva lifted the cup to her lips she said, "My first memory of Esther was when I was two, two and a half. Even though my oldest sister, Harriet, my daughter's namesake, took care of me when our mother was working, it was Esther who never left my side." I could see Minerva struggling to recall distant memories. "We went along as most did back then, secure within our own walls but often vulnerable outside of them." Her face darkened as she continued.

"But back to my sister. We all loved Esther. Oh, we had our spats like any family did. I remember when I was twelve my sister, Anne, got angry at her for talking to her young man who had come for a visit. After he left, she started yelling."

Minerva shook her head seeming to relive the impact of that moment. "Oh, it was terrible the things she said. I was standing off to the side stunned at Anne's anger. I remember my mother came in from the garden just as she shouted, 'You're not even one of us. Your white mother didn't want you and dumped you here after you were born!'

"My mother stormed right over to Anne and slapped her face. Even in her anger I could see my mother was trying to control herself. She took a step back from my sister and said, "Go to your room. Now! Esther ran outside, crying. I started to go after her, but my mother stopped me."

As she spoke, my eyes pooled with tears, a sob caught in my throat.

She patted my shoulder and said, "Don't worry. They made their peace. My parents made sure of that." Minerva chuckled. "Now, where was I. Oh, yes. My mother, sweet as could be, gently cupped my face and said, 'Go and see how Anne is doing, will you? I'll go in to her later after both of us have calmed down.'

"I stood at the screen door and watched as my mother found a weeping Esther crouched by the side of our old well. I remember seeing my mother bend down and sit next to my sister. They were there for, oh, I don't know how long. I couldn't hear what was being said, but when she was done Esther appeared more at peace. When I saw them coming in, I quickly went in to check on my sister, Anne, who by the way did *not* want to see me or anyone else." Minerva smiled at the memory.

Completely lost in a past that came to her new, she continued. "I had never seen my mother raise a hand to any of us. Later, before we went to bed, we were called into the living room. My brother, Simon, and sisters, Harriet and Ruth, were no longer living at home so it was just me, Anne, and Esther. A sullen Anne sat across from me. I could tell she was still angry, but she knew she had to sit there, especially since my father was the one who called us in. Esther, head down and tears spilling down her face, was tucked safely in between our parents.

"Over the next hour my mother lovingly and discreetly spoke about a tragic event that led to an unnamed white girl's ultimate sacrifice. I'll never forget the words my father spoke. With a final authority that none of us would ever challenge, he said, 'Esther is our daughter. She is your sister.' Looking directly at Anne he then said, 'Do you understand?' Anne's soft and tearful, 'Yes' not only closed out the family meeting but sealed further details from ever coming out."

I sat, stunned and amazed at the impossibility of it all. I finally said all I could say, "But, how?

Minerva looked at me like a mother would, reached out and took my hand. "Alice, God is always at work. And trust me, He's not done yet."

I thanked her for her candor and left.

For the next week I struggled with what I now knew and avoided Minerva at all costs. Edith had resumed her distance from life, not once crossing the barrier she hid behind. We lived a separate life, cordial, but somewhat cold.

One morning as I watched her struggle to make her bed I took a chance and crossed the barrier. "Aunt Edith, can I help you with that?"

Looking over at me she weakly said, "Yes."

She stood for a moment clutching the bedspread then sat. Her face began to speak before I heard words. "Alice, tell me."

My heart pounded out *don't,* but I knew she needed, had a right, to hear the truth no matter what. I pulled her vanity chair up close but not invasive. "Aunt Edith, I know I had no right, but I couldn't stand seeing you in such anguish. I spoke to Minerva and what she shared tells me that Esther is indeed your daughter."

Edith took in the words with a breath. In a deliberate exhale Edith said, "Please continue."

I relayed everything Minerva had shared with me as gently as possible, stopping whenever I sensed my words were too painful. As I spoke, Edith kept her eyes on the small wooden bird that now sat on her nightstand. She never interrupted me. When I was done, I handed her a tissue. "Is there anything…I can get you? Do for you?"

Edith reached out for my hands and held them. She met my gaze and smiled. "You have done everything I could never do. Thank you."

That next week I gave Edith plenty of room to process what she had learned. A few times it appeared she wanted to ask me something but withheld her questions. I spoke to Minerva about my conversation with my aunt wanting to prepare her if Edith had questions.

"Alice, that's wonderful. After I prayed, I felt not to share anything with Esther right now, not before I spoke with Edith."

I hesitated to ask but for Edith's sake it was necessary. "Is Esther—well? Does she live close by? Is she married? Have children?"

Minerva held up her hand and laughed. "Hold on. Hold on. There's a lot to catch you up on." She thought for a moment and said, "Should we wait until Edith is present?"

I thought for just a moment and said, "I'm sorry I can't wait. If I'm going to encourage Edith to know more and maybe one day meet her daughter I have to know what she might be walking into. Things like is Esther angry she was left with your sister? Does she blame her mother for the decision she made?"

“I see. Let’s go into the living room. I have a book of old photographs you can look at. Maybe seeing her will put you at ease.”

Minerva ushered me into the small but comfortable room and told me to sit on the couch. She rummaged through a mahogany dresser that sat in the corner.

“Ah, here it is.”

She pulled out an old album and brought it over. As she opened the pages, I could see she was reliving her past with her siblings.

“Here. This one.” She pointed to a black and white photo of a woman surrounded by five children. It was clear she was carrying another by the way her blouse draped over her protruding stomach.

“That’s me in there” pointing to her mother. “I was born around one month later.” Her hand moved gently over the picture as her memory brought it to life. “There’s Esther, the smiling one peeking out from behind my mother’s skirt.” Minerva handed me the album so I could get a closer look.

“What a beautiful family.”

“Esther was such a cheerful little thing. She had a pleasant way about her, always willing to help. Oh, we had our squabbles over the years like any siblings and that one time, I told you about that, when my sister, Anne, thought she was trying to take her boyfriend, which by the way, Esther would never do.”

Minerva moved the book closer to me and turned the pages. “Here’s Esther when she was seventeen, the day she graduated from high school. Oh, Mamma was so proud of all of us. She said education was the way out. Didn’t understand when we were younger but as we grew, we did.”

A few more pages and Minerva said, “Here is Esther on her wedding day. May 16, 1958. It was such a beautiful ceremony." The picture was of a beaming Esther beside a handsome man in a suit. She wore a mid-length lace dress with a demure scoop neckline. Tied at the waist with a wide satin ribbon, the dress accentuated her small waist.

"Our mother made that dress. Made all us girls our wedding dresses."

I handed the book back to Minerva. My next question came with reservations. "But...how has her life turned out? Where is she now?"

Minerva smiled and closed the book. "Esther is doing just fine. A few years ago she moved to De Soto, Texas, when her husband's father got cancer. Frederick's mother was infirmed, so they wanted to be there to help. It's hard having them so far away, but we write and talk often." Minerva paused and closed the book.

"She has children, six of them living. Let's see...a boy, James, born a few years after they married. They lost one the next year, another boy, but a girl, Sarah, was born in, oh, in '65 then a son in '69. Named William. Her and her husband added to their brood when Fred's sister and her husband died, tragic it was, and left three small children. Esther didn't hesitate and took them all in. She was always generous like that." Minerva opened the album again and turned to the next to the last page.

"Here." She handed it to me, and I saw a beautiful family all standing together dressed in their Sunday best.

"This was Easter Sunday. Just before they all moved to Texas. That was years ago, though."

"This is wonderful. Thank you for sharing these pictures with me." I started to hand her back the book, but she stopped me.

"Do you think it would be a good for your aunt to see these?"

I couldn't hold back my tears and said, "I think it would be wonderful."

1982

"Please, Mom, can I go?" Carli had been begging me to let her go to the movies with her friends for months now.

"Let me think on it. Okay?"

"You never let me go anywhere by myself!"

The slam of her bedroom door signaled to me to leave her alone for a while. Edith poked her head out of the kitchen. "Is everything okay?"

"Everything's fine, Aunt Edith. Just a ten-year-old who wants to be twenty."

"I heard she wants to go to the movies? I'll take her if you want."

"I'm not sure she wants either one of us to take her anywhere. It's not that I have anything against ET. It's just that the group she wants to go with is older, and from what I hear, a bit wiser too."

"How does she even know them?"

"Carli joined the school's writing club. There's only one other girl from her class, two others in sixth grade, even one eighth grader. Guess watching me scribble in my journal has rubbed off on her."

It had been a rough few years. I guess I was naïve about how meeting her Uncle Carlos would affect her. Life had aged him. He wore its disappointments on his tired face, a sad discontentment apparent even to my young daughter.

Looking back, I never should have brought her to the coffee shop where we met up. After a tense hour where Carlos spent most of his time staring into his coffee, we said a weak goodbye.

On the way home, Carli finally asked, "Mom, why was Uncle Carlos so sad? He didn't seem happy to see us, especially me."

I ached for my daughter. "Honey, Carlos *was* glad to meet you. Really. It's just he's made some bad choices and now he's living with the unfortunate consequences of them."

I could tell Carli was thinking over what I had said. "You know, Mom. You sound just like a grown-up." For the first time that day she smiled, and I knew that even at her young age she understood. We both did.

I didn't hear anything more from Carlos until four months later when I received a phone call. It was Mira.

"Alice? It's me, Mira."

"Mira! I can't believe it's you. How are you? I've missed you."

After a brief silence she said, "I've missed you too. Alice…he's gone."

"Gone? Who's gone?"

"Carlos. He died. Was killed."

"What? When?"

"I got a call last night. They found his body under an overpass in Brooklyn. The police said it must have been a drug deal gone bad."

I was stunned but strangely not surprised after our last meeting. Mira's soft weeping brought me back.

"Mira, I'm so very sorry." What was there to say?

"Did Carlos tell you we had been living together for the last few years? We hooked up one New Year's Eve and just sort of stayed together. I knew things had gotten really bad but…guess I just didn't want to think about it."

Sounded familiar.

"Mira, what will you do now?"

"I called my parents. They said to come home."

"That's great, Mira. You need to have some kind of support system right now. Trust me, I know."

"Support system? You sound so…adult." We laughed at the irony of it all.

"Will you stay in touch? Please? And stay safe?"

"I will. I promise."

But we both knew it was a promise she couldn't keep. A few weeks later I read in the paper she died of an overdose. They found her body under the same overpass where Carlos died.

Carli hadn't taken the news of her uncle's death well. I knew I hovered, became fearful. I realized too late it wasn't good for a mother to look too closely at her daughter as she grew, to ease into the sound of her conversations. It's too painful, hanging there, waiting for a signal that you're welcome. I misinterpreted the urge—pushing, this time, into her life. But in my defense my own doubts about my ability to be a good mother were reinforced by a world that had gone crazy. The year began with Ozzy Osbourne biting the head off of a live bat and now news of Tylenol being laced with cyanide. What was next?

One day when I was over at Minerva's I expressed my concerns. "And she thinks I don't understand her, don't trust her."

"Alice, I went through some of the same things with Harriet. Yes, she had a rough patch but look at her now. She's a wonderful mother, on her way to becoming a nurse too. Just trust Jesus, and he'll help you both during this trying time."

"But that's just it, Minerva. How can I trust someone I don't even know?"

"Very true. Then why don't we do something about that this Sunday? There's going to be a visiting speaker. He's gone through a lot before giving his life to Christ."

She saw my hesitation and said, "Do you trust *me*?"

With everything we had been through these last years, she knew I did. I smiled and nodded.

"Good. Then I'll see you and Carli, Edith too if she'll come, at 8:30. We can all go together."

I was the only one who ended up going to church with Minerva. Edith was feeling poorly so Carli offered to stay home with her, an offer that came quickly when the other choice was church.

I had never been in a church like that. Young and old, black, white, and brown mingled freely with each other, smiling and hugging like it was one big family. Once we found a seat, I glanced over at Minerva who hadn't stopped grinning since we walked in the door.

She turned to me, patted my hand and said, "I know. I know. It can be overwhelming at first but just sit back and relax and open your heart and mind for whatever God wants to do.

Did she know that's what I was afraid of?

After a time of loud and joyful singing, the pastor introduced the speaker. "Friends, today we are honored to have with us Joseph Clarke. Some of you are familiar with this anointed man's story of redemption and healing after reading his book, *After the Storm*. He motioned to the side of the stage and said, "Joe, I hand over the pulpit to you. God bless you."

He wasn't what I expected for someone speaking at a church. Dressed in faded jeans and a blue and white plaid shirt, no tie, he walked over to the pastor and shook his hand. His curly brown hair looked a bit unkempt and his beard could have used a trim.

"Good morning, all. Thank you Pastor Michaels for that wonderful introduction. The redemption Pastor spoke of came freely by God's grace but the healing—the healing came much slower and to be honest is still going on today."

I leaned over and quietly said, "Minerva, he looks uncomfortable up there."

"Don't worry, dear. He'll be fine once he gets his bearings."

Joe shifted his notes and continued. "Some of you have read my book and know my story and the story of my family. For those of you who don't and are probably wondering who let the homeless man in, I assure you this version of me you see up here is a thousand times better than what it used to be."

Polite laughter and agreeing nods lightened the mood, signaling to those who indeed thought someone had let a homeless man in that all was as it should be.

"I was brought up in a home where alcohol and abuse went together like bread and butter. My father had been raised with anger and cruelty so it was natural for him to raise his children the same way. My mother tried the best she knew how but eventually drank herself to death when I was ten. My sixteen-year-old sister ran away from home two weeks after our mom died, leaving me with a father who found a way to blame me for my mother dying and my sister leaving. Blame can be like poison to a young mind."

My heart pounded out the words—blame like poison; distant memories, toxic and intruding, began to force their way to the surface.

Joe continued. "When I was twelve, he told me to pack a suitcase. That afternoon, my father took me to his brother's house and just drove away. I never saw him again.

"My uncle was a drug addict who introduced me to a world where I began to lose myself and my, my..." His voice cracked. “Excuse me, please.” He took a sip of water and continued.

After a brief pause he said, “But this morning I won’t dwell on the hurtful past. Today I’d like to talk with you about understanding the purpose to the pain we carry.” He held up his palm and said, “I know, I know. Not exactly what you might have wanted to hear today, but I pray that my words would minister to you no matter what kind of pain you’re going through, whether it’s physical pain, emotional pain or relational pain.”

He moved away from the pulpit as he spoke. “When we’re in any place of unrelenting pain and anguish trying to understand the purpose for it all feels unattainable, doesn’t it?

“But as with any storm, there is a place within, an eye, where calm resides. Think of a tornado where the calm is surrounded by a chaos whose only purpose is to consume and destroy.

“As you know, that calm only comes from our Jesus, but the question is how to find this place where we can find rest and the purpose for the pain.”

He lowered his head. “Strange to hear the words rest and pain in the same sentence, isn’t it?” Continuing he said, “As God began to work through my own pain He showed me there are different levels of purpose that He allows in our lives like the layers of an onion, some so thin they seem to blend in with the ones beneath it.”

His words made me want to run, run from his pain, run from my pain, run from the pull I began to feel.

“One level is the one where we ask why. It is when we feel ourselves being consumed by something we can’t fix ourselves. This is a time when we are being presented with the opportunity to see beyond the why and see into the present-tense of the moment. It’s there we begin to live and thrive in the space between breaths—the place not of the "I can't" but of the "I Am." It's where the why becomes the Who.

"Another level of purpose is the bigger picture of pain, the one that drives us to our knees because there's nowhere else to go. Something I know very well.

"This is where we look for the big purpose of our pain. We say grand things like, 'God will use this pain for my good and for the good of another.' Yes when you give your life over to God this is true, but because it's not the present we live in, we can become discouraged for the waiting. It's there we learn to drive ourselves deeper into His grace. Faith matures here more than in any other soil. It trains the eyes of our hearts to see into the eternal places where the truth of 'All things work together for good' becomes a living reality.

"Another level is the effect our pain has on those around us, how it touches those who love us. We begin to understand that our pain is their pain, harder to bear because the journey through the storm is one that, like our salvation, must be first done alone."

Our pain is their pain. My life was becoming undone.

"This is when our spirit-man has the opportunity to grow beyond itself and take the eyes that are fixed on Jesus to see into another's heart. It is where our focus learns to shift outward. God's purpose in anything we go through is to always drive us deeper with Him, deeper into the knowledge of His character."

Joe paused and closed his eyes. He took a deep breath, looked up and scanned the congregation as if looking for someone.

Did he see me? Did he know me?

"The purpose for the seasons of pain we go through? As with all things, God desires to take and mature our faith, bring us into a fuller relationship with Him and drive us deeper into His arms."

He closed his Bible and said, "During those times, we need to release our burdens; relinquish the past and all its injustices because all that extra baggage…"

His voice had become almost a whisper. I don't remember anything after his words "extra baggage." I closed my eyes and tried to desperately hold back my tears.

I will not break. Not here. Not now.

I was brought back with his final words, "Thank you all for listening, and may God bless and keep you."

Minerva smiled and hugged her way down the aisle while I just wanted to disappear. Joe's words still pounded at me, invaded me, demanding an agreement I was unable to give.

As we neared the back of the church, I panicked. He was there, shaking hands with appreciative parishioners. Minerva went right over to him, offering her hand.

"Mr. Clarke, your story, your words touched me deeply this morning. Thank you for sharing your heart with us. My family and I would love to extend a dinner invitation if you don't have other plans."

"Joe, please. It's always an honor." Looking over at me he said, "Actually I don't have any plans later. I'd love to accept your very generous invitation."

After Minerva gave him her phone number and address she moved away leaving me standing there exposed and vulnerable.

"And who might you be?"

Why is he speaking to me? Can't he see I just want to get out of here?"

"I'm…I'm just Alice, Minerva's neighbor." I shook his hand lightly and bolted to the door.

He good-naturedly called after me. “Hey, just Alice, will you be at dinner tonight too?”

I turned to see him smile and give a brief wave. My face reddened as I awkwardly raised my hand.

How was I going to get out of this?

Mary Agnes

1984

I pulled back the tent flap, groggy and somewhat disorientated. The rocky peaks of Cradle Mountain, clouds low and misty, faintly touching, loomed in the distance. Zelda, one of the hitchhikers we picked up yesterday and who I was certain was now sharing Oliver's sleeping bag, smugly told me Cradle Mountain was named because of its resemblance to a miner's cradle, a rocker box used to separate the gold from the dirt. I squinted at the rocky peaks. S*eparate gold from dirt. Which one was I*?

I had gotten drunk again last night, all to the delight of our new "friends." I heard Oliver's voice behind me, low and seductive, words I knew were not meant for me.

I stepped from the tent, not wanting to disturb others I barely knew, crammed into bags, heads hidden, cocooned. I let out a sigh and saw my breath. We had pulled the caravan over last night and set up the tent, not sure of exactly where we were. The sun barely rising, a slight glint finally promising sun. It had been raining the past two days casting a gloom, at least for me, on our trip.

The view made me feel small, insignificant, unworthy of its majesty. I heard rustlings in the tent, a female laugh and then silence. *What was I doing here?*

I met Oliver Watts a few months ago. Two years younger than me, he was a fascinating mix of intelligence and spontaneity. Why he sought me out was a mystery. I wanted to believe he found me attractive, interesting even. But looking back I realize his attraction was due to the fact I was a good listener. I listened as he talked about his career goals. I listened as he bragged about his achievements. I listened, never interrupting, something way too familiar. *Hadn't I honed this skill with Richard*?

The last day of the term, Oliver came into my small office, grabbed my hand, and began to dance me around the room.

"Oliver, what are you doing? I'm working…"

"I'm dancing with you, Mary. Dancing you all the way to Australia." He twirled me and bent me over in an awkward dip.

"Stop. Please." I straightened my shirt and smoothed my hair. He smiled, smirked actually, and half sat on the corner of my desk. I pulled out my chair and sat, giving me the distance I needed.

He folded his hands and took a breath. "I'm *going* to Australia."

"How nice for you, but I don't know what this has to do…"

"I want you to come with me."

"Come with you? Oliver, what…"

"I'm travelling to Australia next month." He sounded casual like "I'm going to the store later." Was it to impress me?

"Never been. Thought it would be fun, an adventure." His smile began to file me down. I looked at him, perhaps seeing him, really seeing him for the first time. His dark brown bangs hung loosely over one eye, giving him an air of mystery, like a well-groomed pirate. His eyes, dark like his hair, deep and searching, bore into me. Did I imagine their intent?

I looked down at some papers to break the tension growing in my chest and said, "Oliver, you're telling me you're going to Australia and you want me—*me* to take off work for what, for how long?"

"Two weeks."

"For *two weeks*, taking what vacation time I have, leaving my, my…"

He leaned over, placed his hand on the papers I was using to distract me, and whispered, "Leaving your what?"

He had a point.

My flirt with adventure left me emptier than I thought possible. I now knew there was a world out there with wild-haired free spirits named Zelda, mountains conquered by fearless explorers, and untamed places like Blowhole and Devil's Kitchen. I was caught in a rocker, baptized in a torrent of water seeking gold, being tossed by dirt and looking for anything of value.

Last year after reading about Richard's engagement to a younger, blonder version of myself, I went into my bedroom, pulled down the shades, draped a sheet over the top half of my full-length mirror so that just my legs were showing, and slowly raised my skirt. As I gazed into the fragmented image of my reflected other, I pretended there was someone else fixed, hidden beneath the sheet, someone who, when I pulled back the covering, wouldn't feel small and insignificant under the height and weight of the disjointed narrative that was my life.

Alice

1986

I had been concerned over Edith's weight loss and increasing fatigue over the past few months. When she finally agreed to go to the doctor, the news was devastating but not a complete surprise to either of us. The tense silence that hung in the air during the ride home was oppressive, preventing me from speaking.

While we were stopped at a traffic light, Edith nonchalantly said, "I'd like to go to church with you and Carli this Sunday if that's alright."

I held the hallelujah in and calmly said, "That would be wonderful, Aunt Edith."

My daughter was excited when I told her Edith would be joining us. Carli had gotten involved with the church's youth group and had finally begun to see past her anger and give God a chance. There was a light now that replaced the darkness I feared would consume her.

My friendship with Joe Clarke had progressed to where he was a regular guest at Sunday dinner. At first Carli was restrained in accepting Joe as part of our lives, but she eventually realized he wasn't a threat. She had even begun praying with him about *her* pain, something I found it difficult to do.

"She's really coming?" asked a surprised Carli.

"She said she would."

In my daughter's young wisdom she said, "Better start praying now."

The sanctuary was packed. Edith hesitated as she walked in the door. I felt her stiffen beside me, so I gently placed my arm around her shoulder and said, "It's okay. Everyone here is friendly." I smiled at her and said, "They won't intrude unless, of course, you want them to."

Edith smiled back and relaxed. I chose seats somewhere in the middle not wanting to add to her discomfort.

Carli said, "Aunt Edith, you'll like it here. Mom, before it begins I'm going to say hi to Amber if that's okay."

I nodded, glad for the time alone with Edith. After my daughter left I asked, "How are you doing?"

Edith slipped off her coat and said, "A little overwhelmed, but I'm all right as long as you're by my side."

The service began with a mix of worship songs and hymns. When people clapped to the songs, Edith glanced at me as if to say, "Is that allowed?"

"The worship can get a little…lively, but don't worry, it's still respectful."

Pastor Michaels stepped up to the pulpit, praising God as he took the microphone. "Good morning! We welcome all who have come before and all who are here for the first time. As it says in Ephesians 1:18-20, 'I pray that the eyes of your heart may be enlightened in order that you may know the hope to which he has called you, the riches of his glorious inheritance in his holy people, and his incomparably great power for us who believe. That power is the same as the mighty strength he exerted when he raised Christ from the dead and seated him at his right hand in the heavenly realms.'"

Edith looked around confused when people voiced their agreement with a loud, "*Amen*!" I patted her hand which she had placed in mine once we were seated.

He began. "Hope. Are you in need for some of God's holy hope today? I know I am."

Edith shifted in her seat and leaned forward ever so slightly. I prayed his words would draw Edith in, ministering to her doubts, her questions, and her fears.

"I want you to imagine a person standing on a beach. This person represents us as we stand before the unlimited majesty of the Almighty God and the choice to accept salvation. Imagine the water represents being immersed into the Christian life. The distance to which we are willing to go out toward the invisible horizon and the depth we are willing to reach represents our walk and the level of our commitment to God. Well, today is the day you decide to step off the beach and enter the water of salvation. This is the first step. Who is ready to make that first step today? It all begins here."

I could feel Edith shift in her seat again. I prayed she wouldn't bolt for the door, something I had entertained once or twice since the sermon began.

The pastor continued. "Once the decision to enter the water is made, questions begin to surface: Do I really need to venture out past my comfort zone and wade out toward the unknown? Can't I just be saved without going deeper?"

My heart began a familiar pounding in my chest. Carli and I had made the decision for God, but I was slow in giving up control in certain areas of my life.

"You see, as we stand in the shallow water, we are in no danger of drowning. We can stand on our own two feet, and can get out of the water without much trouble. But in the shallows is where the breaking waves push and pull at us, sapping our strength. The longer we stand there, the deeper our feet sink into the wet sand like anchors. We are stuck, and we get tired." Pausing, he asked, "Are you tired today?"

He walked back and forth, occasionally stopping to make a point before some unsuspecting parishioner.

"You know, I spent a lot of time metaphorically in the shallows in my Christian life. I was in the water, I was saved, but because my trust in God was limited and because there was no real depth or grounding to my understanding of His nature, I was afraid to venture out to a place of uncertainty. I would inwardly laugh when I'd hear Christians recite Matthew 11:28, 'Come to me all who are heavy laden, and I will give you rest.' 'What rest,' I'd say. 'I'm exhausted.' But there was always this gentle, small voice calling me deeper.

"Where are you today? Are you on the beach, waiting and wondering if you should take the next step and enter in? Are you standing in the shallows, anchored to an exhaustive existence? Or are you yearning to go out toward the deep?"

I wasn't sure how Edith was receiving all this but his questions challenged me, pulled at me. He walked to the side of the stage and came down the stairs into the center aisle.

"Intimacy with God is not an experience that happens *to* us. It is a state of being, a state of existence that develops *within* us. As we allow God into our inner man, we are drawn deeper into His presence. It is when we place ourselves *in* Him, not near Him or around His people, that we can truly be intimate with God and live in Holy Hope.

"But why the need for such intimacy with God you might ask? Why not just a little depth? Can't you just know of God and allow Him to be a part of your life, even the most important part of your life? When I was younger I remember my old pastor asking the question, 'How many here have Christ as the most important part of their life?' I smiled and proudly raised my hand. Was I surprised when he then said, 'Christ should not be the most important part of your life. He should be your life.' I had missed it. It was the difference between acting like a Christian and being a Christian. Too many times I had diminished my Christianity with a compartmentalized attitude—God goes here, work goes there and so on. No wonder my walk was a series of up and down emotionally-driven experiences."

He paused as if searching for the next word. Continuing down the aisle he said, "So...you finally decide you're tired of living on the shoreline and venture out a little deeper. You get past the breakers and find that you're up to your neck, hanging out managing the waves like I did. You decide it's nicer out here, no pushing and pulling, floating around, jumping over small waves. You wonder could this be what God meant when He called me deeper? You might even be tempted to think that even though I can still stand on my own feet, I'm much deeper than I used to be and certainly much deeper than those people over there on the shore.

"However, there's a problem. Some people stay here in their Christian lives. They get to a place of beginning trust with God, a place of learning, living deeper than they used to, even getting through some big trials, but for whatever reason, they decide not to go any deeper.

"But the gentle voice of the Spirit will always call us on to a place of unnatural depth because it's there we must totally depend on the supernatural sustaining power of God, and it's only in that state of total dependence will we be able to form a consistent, lasting, intimate and hopeful dependence on the Father.

"Now, stay with me, dear friends. Picture yourself answering the call to go deeper. You start to swim out to where you cannot stand on your own anymore. You've left most of your friends behind, so there's no one to grab onto when you get tired. You decide to tread water for as long as you can and resist the Spirit's urging to just let go and sink into the depth of the Father's love and care. You finally come to the end of your strength and release yourself into God's hands.

"When you go under the water, you immediately notice the world appears much different than on the surface. The noise of the world is muffled and distant. The burning, hot sun is diffused and cooled. You hold your breath for as long as you can, but your lungs are ready to burst. You see, in a natural sense, your body wasn't made to exist beneath the water, just as your old man, your natural man, cannot sustain you in the deep of your Christian life."

Pastor Michaels walked back to the side of the stage and leaned against the half-wall.

"At this point, you have three choices. One, go back to the shallows and spend your life getting slammed by life's trials, being pushed and pulled by the world's current. Two, go back to the surface where you can breathe on your own and spend your life treading water, never enjoying the intense pleasure and rest that comes from living in the deep with God.

"Or three, listen to the voice that tells you to lean into the breath of God where to live is to depend upon His life-giving grace, respond to the call that urges you toward the intimate sustaining embrace that is hidden from those who exist on the surface, and discover the joyful worship that springs up from the depths of your inner man. It is here that hope springs eternal.

"Living hope means to live in the depths with God, to seek out His will, His heart, and His love. It means to live in the hope-full reality of God's Truth, not in the hope-less misleading of haphazard circumstances."

His voice grew with strength and conviction. "What is the truth? You can do all things through Christ who strengthens you. You are loved, you are provided for, and you are rescued. The truth is you are protected, redeemed, forgiven, restored, and chosen. You have been given beauty for ashes.

"To live hope means to daily take a stand to remember not only who God is, but who you are in Christ. To live hope means to believe the Word of God and to speak the Word of life into situations the world would consider hopeless. The bones are dry and dead, but the breath of God restores. To live hope is to live in Christ because He is the Truth that covers and revives us.

"To live hope is to live in the promises of God, not in circumstances or worldly standards and judgments. To live hope is to be attached and nourished and sustained by the very hand of God, to be cradled in His embrace, free to take flight like the eagles, to stand on the heights like the deer, and to dance like the angels." The congregation enthusiastically voiced their agreement.

He raised his hand and said, "What is Holy Hope, my friends? It is the light when everything around you is in darkness. It is the rest when the noise of the world tries to disturb your peace. It is the grace that reaches out to correct the Eden-shift, and it is the agape love of God in action."

He silently walked back up the stairs to the center of the stage. He placed his hand on the pulpit and said, "If you desire to walk with God for the first time or want to dive deeper into His love, please come forward and the elders will pray with you…"

Edith, Carli and I all stood at the same time. Tears of repentance, tears of release, and tears of joy came without embarrassment or shame. And we knew that whatever came next we would be held close in our Father's loving embrace.

Edith

1986

"Alice, can you come in here, please?" Sitting on the edge of my bed I held the open box on my lap. For some strange reason the doctor's words, "Months to live" didn't pierce me to despair, just sounded to me like any sentence would. An extraordinary peace had settled on me ever since as Alice put it, "I got saved." How was this possible? I felt—cushioned, distanced from the hurts that for so long defined me.

Alice poked her head in the door. "Can I get you something?"

"No, dear. Just come in and sit with me." Alice sat close. My, had she grown. She had an innocent way about her now, a child-like faith that filtered through everything she did or said.

I opened Elizabeth's Bible, took out the yellowed envelope tucked between the pages and handed it to her. "Here, will you read this?" Alice looked confused so I said, "My great-aunt, your great-great aunt, gave this to me just before she died. I'm ashamed to say I never did what she asked, at least not until this year. I wanted you to see, read this especially since I'm passing the cabin on to you and Carli." I reached beside me and handed the deed to her.

Alice took both but laid aside the deed. She opened the letter and started to read. "Oh, Aunt Edith, are you sure you want me to read this? It's so personal, just words between the two of you."

"You're right; it is personal, but I wanted you to know that there has been a legacy of praying women in our family, not just…damaged ones." I smiled as I said the words. "Read it out loud to me, please?"

Alice began.

My Dearest Edith,

I had my friend, Mrs. Cortez, write these words to you. You know my old eyes don't work well anymore and what I have to say is too important not to say. Your life has been difficult, I know, but you can take joy in knowing you have allowed life to continue on. It was a hard decision but a worthy one.

Do not turn your face from the only One who can give you peace and bring you to a mature understanding of who He is. He wants to bring you into sweet relationship with Him, especially during those times that challenge. It is then we need to give Him our burdens.

Surrender the past and all the injustice that has been done to you and by you. When you surrender your heart to Jesus, these trials can only drive you deeper into His arms.

My time here is coming to an end, and I'm sorry to leave you but if you drink deep from the well of His living water you will never be alone...

There was more but Alice couldn't continue. She laid the letter down and began to sob on my shoulder. I held her as Jesus held us both.

Felt Like a Sign

Mary Agnes

1987

I needed to go back. I'm not sure why and yet I did. The belief I just wanted to get away from my thoughts and drive out toward the quiet where I could think carried me for only ten miles or so. If I was being honest, I would admit this deep need to go back to where I lost myself, back to where we all lost everything, was something I'd been fighting for years.

Turning onto the narrow dirt road, my stomach mirrored the ruts that had only deepened over the years. As I approached the sharp bend, flashes of the past welled up. I slammed on the brakes, grateful there was no one behind me. An uncontrollable sob broke the surface of my suppressed pain. Time seemed to stop. I was suddenly my fourteen-year-old self, wounded beyond the body, pressed into the still form of my younger sister.

A strange disconnect took over as I stared at a small wooden cross, partially covered by brush.

No!

I almost turned around but felt compelled to go forward. Taking a deep breath, I carefully navigated the last bend at the end of the road and pulled over to the side, intentionally avoiding the cabin.

I turned the car off and sat staring, hands frozen to the wheel. When I finally opened the door, my heart began to hammer against the decision to come, pounding my will almost to a pulp.

I can do this. I need to do this.

I made my way through overgrown brush toward the lake like a dead man walking. Standing at the edge of the beach, I felt the memories rise.

Without knowing why, I began to run to the water's edge. I stopped just short of the water, bent down and took off my shoes, an almost-ritual of surrender.

I never could forget the pottery hot feel of the mud that coated the shore around the lake. Even now as I step into the warm thickness, my feet ooze reminiscent brown clay and settle like filial anchors into the lake's muddy bosom. Why did I come back?

As I stood at the edge, the breeze brushed against my cheek, Judas-like, blown like a kiss from the forest's craggy mouth, parted and speaking back betrayals left there and forgotten until now. Tall, bearded evergreens wandered mirror-close to the water and split between worlds. Their pointed spires shot downward into some calm other-world and carried my aroused guilt beneath the surface.

The water, fetal in its attraction, lapped at my feet and licked the half-dried clay from my toes. Like one who moves out of habit, I walked over to the weathered pier and hesitated.

It would be too much, going to the end of the small dock like before, lying on my stomach, peering off the edge into the fluid face of my reflective other. To stir that reflection into disparity would unsettle this deluded memory.

I turned my back on the water and began to walk toward the cabin.

The trail seemed almost submissive in the narrow way it just laid there, waiting for me. The woods crowded me now. Their branches reached like poor arms reaching for alms across my path. Memories are laid before me like apologetic roses, chilled and chastised.

I focused on my feet—one step, just one more step. At the end of the trail, I reluctantly looked up and stopped short.

The cabin! It almost looks just like it did the last time we were all here together.

There were lace curtains in the windows and two wicker rocking chairs on the porch. What should have been an overgrown dilapidated cabin was a beautiful home, complete with flowers growing in boxes.

How is this possible?

Something sitting on the porch rail made me stop. Covered almost completely in dirt, I saw the worn brim of Frankie's favorite baseball cap given to him by my father before he died. I went over to the porch and reached up for it. As I wiped away some of the dirt, I was brought back to the day when my father placed the hat on six-year-old Frank's head saying he got it to celebrate one of the greatest players he'd ever seen, Willie Mayes.

"Now it's yours, son. Always remember to never let anything or anyone stop you from your greatness."

How?

Raising my clenched fist into the air I shouted, "What am I doing here?" I threw the cap away, distancing myself from the pain. My sobs filled the silence, assaulting the natural hush around me. Spent, I closed my eyes, took a deep breath of the pine-scented air and swallowed whole the blighted memory that had taken all of our childhoods.

It was time to go.

"Mary?"

I let out a scream. Turning to the sound, I was shocked to see the sister I had so often tried to forget. "Alice! What are you doing here?"

Alice came from around the corner of the cabin. Even though it had been years, I would have known her anywhere with her frizzy red hair and freckles.

"I come here all the time. A good place to write."

She tried to sound nonchalant, but I could tell the surprise of seeing me unnerved her. Unable to think of anything appropriate to say, I muttered, “I didn’t see your car.”

“Parked down the road. Stopped to see the Griffins.”

“The who? What?”

“The Griffins. Met them a few years back.” Alice walked over to where I had thrown the cap. She picked it up and brushed it off.

“Alice! I haven’t seen you in, oh I don’t know—in over twenty years? And now you tell me you’re here to see people I’ve never heard of?”

“Hey, Mom.” We both turned at the same time. A young girl came through the woods. “What’s going on? I thought I heard someone scream.”

Alice quickly said, “Carli, I’d like to introduce you to your Aunt Mary.”

Prompted by her mother, Carli came over and extended her hand. “Pleased to meet you.”

I just nodded, almost too stunned to speak. “Yes. Yes. Good to meet you too.”

Alice broke the awkward silence and held up the cap. “I found this the other day when I was cleaning out some old brush around the cabin. Couldn’t believe it.” She looked at me and smiled. “Felt like a sign.” As she walked over to the porch she said, “Mary, let’s go inside.”

Stunned, I followed Alice and her daughter up the stairs. She opened the door and motioned for me to go in. My legs resisted as I placed my foot on the first step. I couldn’t move.

“Are you okay?” asked Alice.

I looked at her smiling face, upset over her casual politeness. “Am I okay? Are you kidding?”

She came over and put her hand on my shoulder as if to steady me and prompt me to go in. “Come on. It’ll be okay. I promise.”

I followed her like a lost dog looking for its owner. When I walked through the door I just stood there. The living room was still the same but completely different if that’s possible. The couch, sitting in the same place I remembered from when we came there as children, and two new upholstered chairs were placed across from it. The kitchen, simple but updated, boasted a vase of wildflowers on the counter. I knew there were two bedrooms off to the side but there was no way I was venturing down that hall. I turned. “Alice, explain to me all of…this!” I was beginning to unravel.

“Carli, can you make us some tea?”

“Sure mom.”

Alice led me over to the couch. “Mary, sit down. Please”

She plopped herself down in a chair across from me, giving us just enough distance. My heart began to race at the familiar surroundings. I felt myself growing smaller, vulnerable once again, something I swore I’d never feel again. Alice tucked her legs up under her, something I hadn’t seen her do since she was little.

“Where do I start? So much has happened. When was the last time we saw each other?”

“Seems a lifetime ago, Alice. Eve and I thought you were…dead. We could never find you.”

“In a way, I was dead, Mary.” I could see Alice was struggling to put to words the last twenty years. “Well, you know I married Donato.”

“Yes, something we all thought was a mistake but who were we at the time to tell you anything.”

“And I wouldn’t have listened to you anyway. I was travelling full tilt down a road, and I didn’t care where it led.”

I leaned in and whispered, "Where's Donato? I assume he's Carli's father."

Alice lowered her eyes. "Yes, he's Carli's father but—Donato died when she was just a baby."

I looked over at Carli who was humming in the small kitchen as she set the kettle to boil.

Alice noticed my uneasiness and tried to assure me. "Carli knows everything. Had a long and difficult talk a few years back. Was good for both of us." She was silent for a respectful moment. "It was a drug overdose. No surprise to you, I'm sure."

"That's right. I remember Eve saying something about you wanting to come stay with her but her husband wouldn't let you. I think we just put all of that out of our minds. Guilt makes a powerful wall to hide behind. Alice, I'm so sorry we, *I* didn't try harder."

"It's okay, Mary. I ended up moving in with Aunt Edith."

I was embarrassed by the avoidance that had shaped my life. I lowered my head and said, "I'm so very sorry you had no other choice than to go back there with that…that…"

"No, Mary. It was one of the best things I ever did. For me and for Carli."

"Oh, Alice, how can you say that? We both know what she was like. She made our lives hell."

"I know and I'm not saying she wasn't difficult when we were with her, but…"

"Difficult? That's putting it mildly." We both started to laugh whether from nerves or from wanting some kind of release.

Carli brought over the tea on a tray with lemon and sugar. "Here you go, Mom. I think I'll leave you two to get reacquainted. I want to go back down by the lake for a while. Maybe stop back at the Griffins. Just come get me when you're ready. No hurry." Carli came over to me and said, "Aunt Mary, it was a pleasure to meet you."

I stood and hugged her. "And it has been my pleasure to have met you. I hope we'll see each other again soon."

Once she left I said, "Alice, she's delightful. So beautiful and sweet."

"Oh that she is. Although sweet is a strong word to describe her. She is a teenager after all."

Alice handed me a cup. "Now let's get to it."

For the next hour and a half Alice poured her heart out to me. She shared details about her life with Donato, the drugs, the confusion and her decision to call Edith and how things changed throughout the years. She also told me about Edith, her sad past and her current health issues.

"It's so hard to believe that our aunt had gone through so much. We never knew, never understood why she was the way she was. It does explain so much, though." I sipped my now cold tea and looked around. "Alice, the cabin looks just like it did. I expected it to be in ruins."

Alice smiled. "Aunt Edith and I began coming up here years ago. She decided she needed to honor Elizabeth's wish that the cabin be preserved *and* enjoyed. We've had something done each year. Looks great, doesn't it?"

"It certainly does, but Alice, isn't it…hard to come up here, down that same road, the same painful memories?"

Alice put her tea down and moved over to sit beside me.

"Mary, you're right. It was hard at first. The second time we came up here I took a walk alone down to where the accident happened. I brought a small cross with me and placed it around where we…" Tears filled her eyes. "Just a good thing to do, you know?"

I hugged her and said, "It was a very good thing to do."

We talked, laughed, and most certainly cried, especially when Alice began to tell me about what she called her and Edith's salvation. I had never seen her so earnest, so genuine. There was no accusing, no condemnation. Just words that poked at me, gentle but painful.

"Are you and Evie going to come say good-bye to Edith? I know there are things she wants to apologize for."

"I will. We will both come, Alice. I'll explain everything to Eve. At least I'll try."

We sat and talked about our father and grandfather and the wonderful times we had. We even talked about Frankie.

Alice looked at her watch. "It's getting late. Do you want to take a stroll together down by the water before you leave?"

I hesitated thinking it would just be too hard to walk that trail with her once again. But I found myself saying, "Sure. I'd love that."

By the time the sun was beginning to fade we stood by the side of my car hugging. Carli had just returned from the neighbors with a loaf of some kind of homemade bread. We exchanged addresses and phone numbers and with tears said good-bye.

"I'll call you in a few days to set up a time for Eve and me to visit.

"That would be great. But don't wait too long. I think her time is nearing an end."

"I won't. I promise."

Genevieve

1987

"You have to come, Evie." Mary pleaded with her sister. "Alice said she's different now, not as…caustic."

Ignoring the last part I said, "I can't believe you saw Alice. And she has a daughter! Mary, this is just too much."

"I know. I know. To say it was a shock is an understatement."

Mary started talking nonstop about Edith, about Alice, about everything my guilt had never wanted to hear. My grip on the receiver tightened with every word.

"…said she didn't have much time left. Said she has cancer. I know we all hated living with her but it's the right thing to do."

"I don't want to do this, you know. We've all moved on with our lives." *Did I even believe that*?

"Do more than try. I'll pick you up on Saturday and we can go over together. Safety in numbers, right?"

Mary's weak laugh told me she wasn't looking forward to seeing Edith either. "I need to think. I'll call you if I decide to go."

When I hung up the phone time slowed as my heart pounded.

Alice. When Donato died back in '72 and she needed a place to go, I felt terrible but my husband, Arthur, forbade me to open our home to, oh how did he put it, to a "drug-crazed hippie." I never even gave her a chance to tell me she had a daughter. Then she just disappeared. But Alice was always good at disappearing when rejected. Something we've all had in common.

I knew I had to go, do what Mary told me to do—I always did, even when it meant taking the blame and enduring the punishment. It was, after all, the least I could do with surviving and all. So I did what I always did after an uncomfortable conversation—I ate half of the pie I made for dinner and took a drink.

Holding the glass like a hand, I lifted it to my tense mouth, swallowing hard enough to feel the burning make its way down to my despair. I sat and stared at nothing, willing the past to stay there. With a last long sip, I closed my eyes and exhaled, pulled like water spiraling down a drain.

For no particular reason I tossed my head back and forth as my tired face danced side to side in a tense, choreographed succession of no's. I stood before the open bedroom closet as if I was waiting for instructions, hands anchored to the metal knobs like magnets. I don't know how long I stood there staring at the smooth tops of the white, satin-covered hangers. Their firm, shiny heads lined up and clinging to the bar like a row of incessant question marks to which I had no answer. Weighted to the floor, it's as if I had somehow become a depository for the world's existential guilt.

Where did I go?

When I closed my eyes, I could still see Arthur's expensive suits and my plain, plus-sized dresses hanging side by side, barely touching. I sat down on the bed and tried to think of what I would tell our friends.

We just grew apart. No, we're still the best of friends. Yes, I regret we never had children and yes, Arthur is a still good man.

I looked at the crumpled French maid's costume that had fallen into a defeated heap after hitting the picture of Arthur's mother that hung like a chaperone on the wall next to our bed. I closed the closet doors and sat down. As I thought about the last few hours, my head began to ache.

"Come on. It'll be fun." Jean, my friend and confidante, had brought over the latest Fredericks of Hollywood booklet. "It'll spice things up for sure." She giggled like a schoolgirl and handed it to me.

"I'm not sure, Jean. Some of these things are so…so, I don't know what." I started to hand it back to her.

Jean pushed it away. "Keep it. You never know what might come of taking a chance." She giggled again and left me alone with my embarrassment and wavering self-esteem.

Now all I could feel was the burning in my round, heavily rouged cheeks and the insult that filled the always empty pit of my protruding stomach.

As I fell back on the new, satin comforter the phone rang, sending a shrill voice into the air like an alarm, interrupting the silence that hung like a constant in the bedroom.

"Hello?" I said equally startled and annoyed.

"Genevieve, is that you, dear? Did I wake you? This is Mother Bradford."

"No, you didn't wake me. I wasn't sleeping." *Oh great.* The tension in my throat travelled down to my tightly-crossed legs. On the other end of the phone was Arthur's better half—his mother.

"Can I please speak to my Arthur, dear? I'll only keep him for a minute."

"I'm sorry, Mother Bradford, but Arthur's not here; he's working late as usual." It never bothered me when I lied to my mother-in-law. Actually, I quite enjoyed it.

She dragged the word "Oh" out in her whiny but oddly masculine-sounding voice. It's as if her vocal chords contained all the testosterone that had somehow forgot to pass itself on to her only male child.

"Well then, why don't I just tell you what I wanted and you can tell Arthur when he comes home. This will only take a minute."

She mindlessly droned on, humming like an overactive hive, dripping sweet and dangerous. "...and I've noticed lately that Arthur sounds unhappy, dear, maybe you could..."

Like always, I added the expected "uh-huh" and "You're right, Mother Bradford" at the appropriate times. All of a sudden, I let the phone slip out of my hand and fall onto the bed. As if for the first time, I noticed my reflection in the full-length mirror on the back of the closet doors. There I sat, half-naked on the edge of the bed, looking like a three dollar hooker from the neck up and a thirty-eight-year-old, overweight, overwhelmed and frustrated woman from the neck down whose only admirable quality that Arthur considered worth commenting on was my ability to make the "perfect cup of tea."

As I stared at my frozen self in the mirror, Mother Bradford's unremitting voice hammered as if it were an displaced apparition banging on the door of this world looking for the attention it never got while it was alive.

Squinting my eyes, I brought my reflected self into focus. Then, almost matter-of-factly, I took the phone and placed it under the pillow on Arthur's side of the bed. I walked across the room, picked up the maid's costume and began to lay it out on the comforter—first, the black and red lace bodice; then the panties, garters, and black fishnet stockings. I put the "at your service" heart-shaped apron on top of the panties and methodically plucked out the feathers of the flaming, red feather-duster. I let them fall across Arthur's pillow, creating a furry frame for the sound that still managed to muffle its way out from under the covers, giving the empty, lacy seduction a voice.

I wonder if he'll notice I'm not in there.

I looked down at the spiritless form like I was paying my last respects. Walking over to the closet, I yanked open the doors as if they were on fire and grabbed an old raincoat and a pair of running shoes I bought but never wore. As I wrapped the raincoat around me, its coarse fibers rubbed against my skin. It reminded me of Arthur.

I passed by his study and looked in. Was there really a time when I thought his self-centeredness was merely the sign of a confident man and the unwavering devotion to his mother was admirable?

Could it have only been an hour ago I stood here desperate and ridiculous?

The humiliation still flushed my cheeks. When he glanced up at me standing in the doorway frantically waving that stupid feather-duster and saying, "At your service," the look on his face leveled the final blow. I didn't know what had hurt worse—the way he laughed or the fact that he laughed at all.

Staring into the dimly lit study, I remembered the chill as he turned away and snickered, "Very funny. I thought you were in bed asleep?" Then nothing, just the ruffle of papers and the reflected glare of the desk lamp off his glasses as he gawked at his work.

I took a small step into the room and shuddered as the memory took a renewed, shameful bite out of my wilted self-esteem. "I'm leaving now," I said, surprised at how calm and controlled I sounded.

"What? Oh, okay, fine. Could you please be a dear and make me a cup of tea? It'll only take a minute."

All the loaded words that had been firing at my insides for years boiled to the surface. But when I opened my mouth, all that came out was, "Sure, no problem."

I tightened the tie on my raincoat and went into the kitchen. I methodically grabbed the copper kettle and slammed it on the stove. After turning the burner on high, I grabbed my purse, walked to the door and stopped by the mirror. A thin ray of light from Arthur's study unintentionally reached out and almost touched the side of my hair.

I quietly closed the door to our apartment and rang for the elevator. I looked both ways down the hallway, hoping I could get away unseen. Suddenly feeling ridiculous, I tried to smooth the creases in my coat.

What am I doing? What am I doing?

The elevator doors came together with a soft whoosh—an appropriate sense of closure without fanfare. Instrumental music filled up the space making me a little more relaxed until I realized it was once *our* song, "Can't Take my Eyes Off You."

Looking up at the ceiling I shouted, "Are you kidding me?" I threw my bag so hard the compact I always carried flew out and shattered against the wall, leaving glass and powder all over the carpet. I bent down to retrieve my purse and without thinking took out a tissue and tried to remove any trace of my outburst.

I suddenly stopped. Standing up, I lifted my chin and looked straight ahead. As the floors continued to swoosh by, I thought about the lifeless lover sleeping still on Arthur's side of the bed, waiting patiently.

The doors opened—an invitation to move ahead. I took a few small steps forward and placed my hands on the smooth sides, preventing them from closing. Drawing in a deep breath, I gave a quick thought to the empty kettle upstairs, passionately heating up and screaming for attention. I released my hands and stepped back into the smallness of the elevator.

Not like this. I am done running away.

Edith

1987

Images floated, carried on the current of morphine and conjecture. They left me wondering, hollowed out but waiting.

Would she come?

Memories flooded my clouded mind as regret tried to circle me like a ravenous vulture waiting to pick me clean.

She had to come.

I had been moved home, watched over by hospice, Alice, and an unknown ghost. These past months as my body grew smaller my faith had strangely deepened, giving me and Alice a complicated peace.

"Aunt Edith?" Alice gently nudged me. "She's here. They've come."

I slowly opened my eyes. "What? She's here?"

Alice nodded. "Let me prop you up."

I winced as I tried to sit up. Seeing the worried look on her face I said, "I'll be fine. Get me my hand mirror—please. And my comb."

"You look fine. Are you ready?"

I took as deep a breath as I could and held it for just a second. "I'm ready."

Alice went over to the door and motioned. "Please come in. She's been waiting a very long time to see you."

Esther respectfully entered the sick room as Alice left to give us time alone. She came over to the bed. "May I?"

I nodded, unable to speak.

Esther gently touched my wrinkled hand. "I've waited so long to meet you."

All I could say before bursting into tears was, "I'm so sorry."

"Sorry? For what?

"For leaving you, for not being…stronger, braver."

Esther smiled. "You did the bravest thing anyone could do for another—giving life. I grew up in a wonderful home with two parents who loved me and siblings who, even when we disagreed, made me feel like a part of the family."

Just then I heard a small cry from the other room. Alice poked her head in and said, "There's someone else here who would love to meet you. Up for it?"

I looked at Esther, confused.

She gently squeezed my hand. "How would you like to meet one of your granddaughters?"

I was overcome. "What? Yes…please. I'd love to."

Esther went to the door and motioned. Her husband, Frederick, entered carrying a small baby girl. "Our newest addition. She'll be five months old tomorrow. We're all so excited. The adoption just went through last week." Esther lovingly took the baby from her husband. She came over and sat beside me.

As I reached out and touched her, I was brought back to that day forty-seven years ago when I looked down at another who had the same small black curls and skin the beautiful color of wet sand. The circle was complete.

"She's wonderful."

Esther was beaming. "We all think so." She propped the baby up next to me and said, "I'd like to introduce you to Grace."

I forgot my pain as I took my daughter's and granddaughter's hand.

The next hour was wonderful, not just for me, but for Esther and Alice. Words of longing and lament, laced with a bittersweet joy, were shared. Esther told me stories about her family that carried me into a past that was full and rich. These memories soothed my guilt and somehow brought a sacred peace to the room.

When Alice saw I was struggling to stay awake she said, "This has been wonderful, but I think my aunt needs to rest."

"May we come and see you again?" asked Esther.

Unable to speak, I just nodded.

As Esther started to get up from the bed, I grabbed her hand. "I have never stopped loving you, loving your father. You have to know that."

"I never doubted it."

That night as my shallow breath slowed, I willingly released my grasp on this life and was pulled away by an unseen hand into the depths of a God who answered my prayers and saved me from myself.

Helen

1987

Where is that...what?

A distant buzzing intruded, interrupted my haze. I blinked my eyes open and saw my life—an ash tray full of half-smoked Camels, a half-empty bottle of Jack Daniels, and a shot glass with red lipstick smeared across its transparent curves like blood on a windshield—*blood on a windshield*! As regrets surfaced like vomit, I swallowed hard to keep down another night's worth of solitude and a lifetime of bitterness. I glanced in the mirror above my dresser and smirked at the lines, rut-deep, that crisscrossed like highways across my face in no particular direction. I looked around the bedroom, focusing all of my own disgust onto the peeling, yellowed wallpaper.

Vague remembering and fitful coughing had met my mornings for far too many years. I gradually pulled my legs over the side of the bed and sat hunched, my arms tightly wrapped around me. I tried to stand. Without thought, I rubbed my arthritic hands together like I was hatching an evil plan. *Maybe I was.*

I stumbled into the dirty kitchen, went over to the small refrigerator and hit it. The buzzing stopped for an instant but returned to irritate. I laid my aching head against the sticky puke-yellow side.

Pigsty!

Sitting at the small kitchen table, I closed my eyes, willing my past forward, pushing out the certainty of the present. A knock at the door roused me.

"What now?"

I pushed my chair away from me like another person and grunted as I got up. I moved slowly these days, even though I was only…what? Fifty-nine? I paused at the door, holding the knob to steady me. Leaning into the frame I said, "Who is it?"

"It's me, Mom. It's Alice. Can I come in?"

I blinked, willing myself into the present. I pressed my face against the doorframe. "Alice? What…what are you doing here?"

"Please, open the door. I'd like to talk to you."

I unlocked the chain and as I pulled the door open, a strange feeling like being punched in the stomach almost took my breath. I motioned for Alice to come in and sit.

"Place is a mess."

Alice looked around, trying not to let me know how disgusted she was. "It's fine, really."

I sat down on the couch and pushed an old newspaper away, revealing an empty whiskey bottle wedged between the cushions.

"Mom, the reason I've come is to let you know Edith died last week. I thought you would want to know."

"What? Edith…how would you know? I haven't seen or spoken to her since…"

"I've been living with her, Mom. Carlotta and I moved in with her almost fifteen years ago.'

"Carlotta? Who's *Carlotta*?"

Alice paused before saying, "She's your granddaughter."

I disregarded what Alice said and got up, numbly walking into the bedroom. After picking up the bottle from my nightstand, I came back into the room.

Trying to sound casual I said, "Fifteen years, huh?" My hand was unsteady as I poured the drink into a dirty glass. I held it up. "Want any?"

Alice shook her head. “Mom, I’ve tried to get a hold of you for years. Your phone’s been disconnected…”

“Then how did you find me?”

“I met an old friend of yours a few weeks ago. Remember Louis?”

“Louis? That jerk. Left me like all the others. Thought he must be dead by now.” I laughed and swallowed what was left in my glass.

“He’s actually doing really well. Works at the hospital where Edith worked. Does maintenance work there. Got himself clean a few years ago.”

I looked up at my daughter and laughed again.

Alice ignored my reaction and said, “He heard you were in the same place, over on Lyons Street. I came by a few days ago and tried your buzzer but no one answered.”

“Wasn’t here.” I fingered the empty glass. “So what have you been up to?”

“I’ve been good, really good. Like I said I have a daughter. She’s fifteen now, bright but sassy. She knows what she wants in life. Says she’s going to college and become a doctor.”

“A high and mighty doctor. What about you?”

“Well, with Aunt Edith’s help I went to community college and got an associate’s degree. I work in an office now; I like it.”

“Still scribbling in those notebooks of yours? Thought you’d be a writer or something.”

“Oh, I still do. Something for me right now. Mom, we’re having a small memorial service tomorrow. Nothing big. She wanted to be cremated. Just her friends…”

“Friends? Didn’t think Edith had any friends.”

“Mom, she changed over the years. Got…softer. She even had the opportunity to meet her daughter, Esther.”

The mention of Edith's daughter brought out an anger that even I didn't expect. I abruptly pushed my chair back so hard it crashed to the floor.

"Mom, are you alrigh…"

"It's time you left, Alice."

"But Mom, I…"

"Leave!" I walked over to the door and yanked it open. Turning to face a daughter I never really knew I whispered, "You need to leave—now."

Alice looked hurt, but I had no words of comfort. She came over to hug me. I flinched but allowed it.

"It was good to see you, Mom. I know you don't want to hear this but Jesus gave me a new life and He can do the same for you."

I shook my head and quickly closed the door.

Swept Away

Helen

1992

The past five years had been a blur. After Alice's visit, the self-destructive pace that had been my life quickened with an intensity that surprised even me. The news of my sister's death ate at me, at least when I allowed myself to feel. Memories, flashes really, pushed their way to the surface, intruding and convicting.

I hooked up with another man two years ago. It didn't really matter to me who it was. What was important was whether he had a place to live and money to spend. I wanted to lose myself, be where no one knew who I was, knew what I had become.

Ron, a retired truck driver, was older than me by ten years. He was somewhat healthy and active when we first met but after only two years, he was now grizzled with age and booze.

"Watch out!"

Ron swerved back into his lane. I looked over at him, wondering why I ever, why he ever…oh whatever.

"Ron, the roads are icy. Slow down!"

He grunted something and seemed to speed up.

Christmas Eve, a night of new beginnings and family. For me, just another night to go out and get wasted.

I opened my purse and took out the small bottle of whiskey I always kept, just for emergencies. I closed my eyes and gulped down what was left. That's all I remembered until I heard the screaming.

Screaming. I hear screaming. Shut up!

I opened my eyes and realized it was me…screaming. I put my hand up to my face and felt the warmth of my own blood as it ran down my cheek.

Through the broken windshield I saw smoke coming out from the crushed hood, almost split in half by a tree.

Dazed, I looked over at Ron. His face, buried in the steering wheel, was bloody and still.

"Ron, Ron. Wake up." I tried to shake him but an intense pain pierced and stopped me cold. My hand searched for the pain in my chest and felt something sharp—broken shards of my bottle, slick with my blood.

I knew I was going to die, wanted to die, end the nightmare that had been my life.

The night was cold and silent, no one around to comfort or ease me into a waiting afterlife. Snow fell gently through the broken windshield.

As I waited for the end to come, I felt myself slip back to a time, back to the accident that changed my life and killed my son.

Alice

1992

"It's a beautiful tree."

I came over to Joe and put my arm around him. "I believe it's even nicer than last year."

The house was full of warmth and dear friends. Carlotta, home from college, had been in the kitchen with me all day, baking cookies and her favorite carrot bread. Minerva and her granddaughter, Esther Ruth, had come early to help get things ready. Harriet was stuck at work again. We all understood that being a nurse meant filling in when needed.

I leaned against the counter and smiled at all the joyous commotion around me. My life was full.

As if to challenge my contentment, the phone rang.

Carli shouted, "I'll get it." She wiped her floured hands and picked up the phone.

I glanced over at my daughter and mouthed, "Who is it?"

She said something into the receiver and motioned for me to come. "Mom, it's for you." She hesitated then said, "It's about grandma."

I quickly took the phone. I placed my hand over the mouthpiece and told Carli to rejoin the group in the living room. She began to object. "No Mom. I'm staying right here."

I reached out and took her hand and nodded my consent. After a deep breath I said, "Hello?"

"Alice, it's me, Louis. You know from the hospital?"

"Yes, yes. I remember. My daughter said something about my mother?"

"I hate to be the one to tell you, especially on Christmas Eve, but I was down in the ER doing some work when they brought Helen in."

The brief silence—a lifetime in the making.

"It's bad, Alice. She was in a car accident. You should get here as soon as you can."

Stunned but strangely not surprised, I composed myself and said, "I will. Thank you for calling me, Louis." I stood frozen by the phone visibly shaken. Even though this was the call I knew would one day come, I was ill-prepared to have my mother gone.

Joe came over and put his hand on my shoulder. "Alice, you look upset. Is everything okay?"

I turned to my dear friend and said, "No. There's been an accident. My mother…" I broke at the words. My sobs brought the others into the kitchen, all wanting to know what happened as well as to comfort.

My daughter helped me to the couch while Esther brought over a glass of water.

"I have to go to the hospital. Can someone please take me? I…I don't think I can drive right now."

Minerva sat down next to me. "Of course, dear." She looked around at the group and said, "But first, we need to pray."

The group gathered around, hands laid to give strength and comfort. When the time was right Minerva said, "Amen." She took her car keys out of her purse and handed them to my daughter "Could you please warm up the car and brush off the snow?"

Carli hugged me and said, "I'll do it right now."

Within ten minutes we were headed for the hospital. After inquiring at the main desk, a nurse brought us into the busy ICU. When we entered the room, the monitors and IV lines almost concealed my mother's feeble form. I stopped cold and stood by the curtain.

My daughter stepped up to the bed and asked the nurse, "How is she? Will she…wake up?"

Checking the IV she unsympathetically said, "I'm afraid I don't know. There was a lot of damage. You need to prepare yourselves. Call any other family members you need to." She looked down at my mother and said, "You know it's a miracle she wasn't killed." As she left she mumbled something under her breath about damn drunk drivers and walked out.

Carli came over to me and said, "Mom? Did you want me to call Aunt Mary and Aunt Eve? Mom?"

"What? No. I'll do it." I turned to Minerva and said, "Can you please stay while I make the calls?"

"Absolutely. Anything you need me to do. I'm not going anywhere."

Carli pulled up a chair and placed it by the side of the bed. "I'll just sit right beside her."

Thank you, God, for this wonderful daughter.

I went out by the desk and finally found the nurse. "Excuse me. Is there a phone somewhere private I can use?"

"Yes. There's one in the small consultation room." Softening she said, "I'll show you where it is."

I turned back toward the room and saw my beautiful daughter holding her grandmother's bruised hand, eyes closed. Minerva stood behind her with her hands on her shoulders. I knew they were praying.

Mary Agnes

1992

I heard the phone ringing as I fumbled in my purse. To no one in particular I said, "Just a minute. I'm coming." I dropped the keys once but managed to open the door before the phone stopped ringing.

"Hello?"

"Mary, you sound out of breath. Are you okay?"

"Fine. Just got in. I was down at the soup kitchen getting things ready for tomorrow. What's up?'

I had tried to stay in contact with Alice after Edith's funeral but found it hard to put aside the past.

"Mary. It's about Mom."

"Mom? What's she done this time? In jail?" I laughed but knew as soon as I did that it wasn't funny.

Alice ignored my lack of respect. "No. There's been an accident. She's in the hospital. It doesn't look good, Mary."

All the years of avoidance barreled in, taking my breath.

"Mary? Did you hear me?"

"Yes…yes. Tell me where she is. I'll be there as soon as I can. Is anyone with you?"

"Yes. Carli came. She's in with Mom now. Minerva drove us."

I dreaded asking but knew it was necessary. "Does Eve know?"

"No. I called you first."

"Do you want me to tell her?"

I could hear Alice exhale into the receiver. "Yes. Please. That would be…thank you."

Genevieve

1992

The living room was full of friends and neighbors. We had begun inviting people over on Christmas Eve a few years ago after I decided to stop being angry. As provincial as it sounded, marriage counseling had actually made a difference. Even though we yelled and cried and blamed during our sessions, we've slowly made our way back to each other. Arthur admitted his distance and I my dissatisfaction. It's been a slow healing but a healing nonetheless.

When the phone rang, I went into the bedroom and closed the door.

"Hello?'

"Eve. It's Mary."

"Mary! I was thinking of you the other day. I'm so sorry I haven't called. It's just that…"

Mary interrupted. "Eve. Mom's been in an accident. Alice called me. Eve, she's hurt really bad."

With the words "in an accident," I stopped breathing. My vision narrowed and a tidal wave of anxiety washed over me.

"Eve? Did you hear me? Eve?"

Trying to push aside the intense fear that was threatening to swallow me whole I stumbled out the words, "Yes. Yes. I heard you. An accident."

"Alice and Carli are at the hospital. They said we should come right away."

"I…I don't know if I can come tonight. We have guests, a room full of people. We've both had a few glasses of wine. We shouldn't drive." I was rambling and everything sounded like a lame excuse. I knew my reluctance to go to the hospital had nothing to do with the wine.

"I understand, but please try to come as soon as you can. I don't think she's going to pull through, not this time."

"I will. I promise." I hung up the phone, disconnecting myself from my promise.

I wish I could disconnect from my mother and all her drama.

The power I had allowed her to have over me ever since I could remember smothered me new. I had told Mary I would go and see her, but what I really wanted to say was "Payback's a…"

Arthur opened the door. "Everything okay, dear?" He saw the look on my face and came into the room. He sat down next to me and put his arm around my shoulder. "What's the matter?"

I leaned into him and began to sob. "It's my mother…car accident…hurt really bad…have to go."

He would never know how much it meant for him to just let me cry, not try to fix or even console.

"Do you want to go tonight? People will understand."

"We can't. We've been drinking and…"

He grabbed a tissue off the nightstand and began to wipe my tears. "We can call a taxi." He placed a brief kiss on my cheek. "Whatever you need we'll do."

"Thank you. No. We can go tomorrow. I need…time to…"

"I understand. You stay in here as long as you want. I will entertain our guests."

When he left I was somewhat comforted, but anxiety still lingered beneath the surface. I sat on the edge of the bed and stared into the closet mirrors.

I've been here before.

Looking at my reflected self, I saw perhaps for the first time my resemblance to my mother. Unnerved and somewhat disgusted I wondered, *have I become as callous as her too?*

I lay in bed unable to sleep. I looked at the clock on the nightstand—3:00 a.m. I was afraid to close my eyes, terrified I would see it all again…the broken glass, the blood, the crumpled bodies, hear my mother moaning, screaming for me to do something.

The sleeping pill I took began to lower my defenses. Everything I had tried so hard to push down and away for more than thirty years rose to the surface. But this time I would allow it all to come, allow it to swallow me, punish me anew.

November 1961

I am just drifting off to sleep, trying to put the previous scene out of my mind. Mother has lost it again. We've learned to accept her rants and erratic behavior, so we obediently grab what we can and get into the car.

I hear Frankie call "shotgun" even before we open the doors, so as always, Mary, Alice and I cram into the backseat, grumbling as we pull the doors shut.

"I'm cold," whines Alice.

My mother turns and yells, "You know the heat doesn't work." She tries to soften her tone and says, "Just snuggle with your sisters. You like that."

We all did enjoy a good snuggle with Alice but tonight nothing would soothe our troubled minds.

I'm sitting behind my mother. Even though my father has been gone five years now I tell myself I can still detect the faint smell of the cigars he would only smoke in the car, away from condescending remarks.

I settle in for what I know will be a long night. We have been driving for the past hour and even I can see the weather is beginning to turn. My mother has been fumbling in her purse for a cigarette, and I feel the car swerve. I look over at Mary who is holding Alice's hand. My heart hammers in my chest, and the night closes around me.

I start to cry and brave the words, "Mom, you should slow down. The roads look icy." She responds with the characteristic, "Shut up or I'll give you something to cry about."

I take the sweater I grabbed before we left and ball it up against the frosted window, trying to push aside the gnawing feeling that we are headed for disaster. All of the night's drama has taken its toll. I close my eyes against it all and try to slow my breathing. Suddenly, I hear my mother's loud cursing and then—nothing.

A slow awakening. *Everything's blurry. What's wrong with my eyes*? I raise my hand up to my head and feel a warmness that even in my confused state know is not supposed to be there. *Blood*! *My blood*? *What*?

I am on my back looking up at a broken side window. *Why is my sweater hanging there like that*?

I hear a weak moan. I turn myself over just enough to see my sister's crumpled form beneath me. "Mary! Mary! Are you okay?" Nothing.

My head and my arm throb with my heart.

Why am I looking up at my window?

The window, broken and smeared with blood, is now above me. In one horrific moment I realize the car has tipped over and landed on its side. I turn my head sideways and see there's smoke coming out from underneath the car's crumpled hood.

Is that a tree?

The back and forth rhythm of my head sends a shooting pain down my neck.

I scream everyone's name at once… "Mary, Alice, Frankie, Mom!" but no one answers. I grab at Mary and begin to shake her. Nothing.

I hear moaning coming from the front seat. "What's…? No. No! Frankie!"

I try to pull myself up toward the front. That's when I only see the lower half of my brother's body sticking through the broken windshield.

"Mom! Is Frankie all right?" Mom!" I know he's not all right.

My mother moans, "Mary? Alice? Eve, are they…okay?"

I look over at my sisters, but they're not moving. "I…I don't know. They're not awake."

My mother begins to scream and cry again. I am mute with grief and anger.

"Eve. Eve, you have to go for help. Eve!"

I finally mutter, "No, Mom. I…can't. I'm hurt."

"My legs are…stuck. I'm trapped!" Her moans become curses that hit me hard like a slap. Exhausted she finally says, "Evie, you have to go."

"Go where? I don't even know where we are!"

"We're on the dirt road maybe a mile from the cabin." She strains with every word. "We passed a house…back a ways."

"Mom, I can't."

"Yes, you can, Eve. You have to or we're all going to die!" Another slap.

I look up at the window and wonder if I can even fit through it. I grab the back of the seat and try to reach the door handle. Ignoring the pain shooting through my arm I place my hands on the frame of the window. My weight pulls at me and accuses.

I sink back and yell, "I can't!"

More curses. More insults.

Her words cut deep and find their mark, splinter like broken glass into what's left of me. I pull myself up with one last push and sit on the bent window frame, more to get away from her words than to save anyone. The wind swirls around me and revives. For an instant, I am lifted away from everything beneath me.

My mother screams my name again and curses. Falling to the ground in a bloody heap, I stumble away from the car. Dazed, I turn and mindlessly look around. Sleet, like needles, stings my face. I begin walking as if in a dream down the dark, slippery road. My mother's screams for her children to wake become a disappearing noise behind me.

Does anyone care if I wake up?

My heart beats with every step. I start to shiver and can't stop.

Am I cold? *Am I scared*?

I look back. Light fluffy snow is beginning to fall, muffling out the sounds behind me. I collapse to my knees and start to cry. For Frankie? For myself? For a father who isn't here to comfort me?

I numbly place my cut hands on the ground. The cold relieves as the blood accuses, shouts at me to save my family. As I struggle to stand, I see a faint light down the road.

A house? Someone must be home!

I begin to run toward the light. With every step, my heart pounds hard against the deep pain I always carry.

I am not enough.

I finally reach the house and stumble up the stairs. Pounding on the door I yell, "Help! Help!"

Why isn't anyone answering?

After a few minutes I stop and just sink down on the stoop and fall away from everything that is my life. I am shaking again. I pull myself around me and give myself a final, desperate hug.

Wake up!

I feel someone lifting me, taking me inside the light, saying words, asking questions.

"*Help my family, please. Accident. Up the road.*"

That's all I remember until I wake up in a small hospital room. I have been asleep for two days.

"Eve. Eve. Wake up."

"What? Arthur, why are you shaking me?"

"Eve, you were screaming in your sleep."

I sat up and yanked the covers away from me. "I'm fine, fine."

Arthur knew I was lying. He sat next to me and asked, "Do you want to talk about it?"

I looked into his face and saw a man different from even last year. Did I dare speak the words? Could I even put a voice to what I had kept hidden for so long?

"Yes. Yes. I want—need to bring this ghost into the light and send it on its way."

Alice

1992

The doctor said she could pass anytime now. It's been six days since the accident, and she still hasn't regained consciousness. Carli was staying with Minerva and came when she could. Mary visited a few times which gave me time to go home and rest. Eve hasn't come yet but told Mary she would.

I closed my eyes and felt myself begin to drift off when I heard my name.

"Alice?"

I turned to the door and saw Eve. We smiled and I motioned for her to come into the room. She looked at the bed and then back at me. I could see the struggle on her face as she came over and pulled up a chair.

"I'm sorry it's taken me so long to come. I just needed to…make peace with some things."

"I'm just glad you're here now." We chatted about superficial things avoiding anything important.

I looked back towards the bed and said, "Eve, I know how hard this is for you, has been for you. Mom was wrong placing the blame on you for Frankie's…" I stopped and heard Eve's muffled sobs.

"Oh, Eve. I'm sorry. I shouldn't have brought that up."

Eve took out some tissues from her purse and wiped at her eyes. "I've decided to go to counseling to try and work through it all…feeling I was…never enough, like I failed Frankie, like I didn't…" She couldn't continue. We just sat and held each other for a while until the nurse came in to check my mother's vitals.

"Sorry to interrupt."

I suggested to Eve we go and get some coffee. Turning to the nurse I said, "We won't be gone long." She told us not to worry, that she'd keep an eye on things.

We found a quiet corner in the cafeteria. As soon as we sat down Eve said, "Alice, can you ever forgive me for not insisting you come stay with us?"

I looked at my sister's weary face and said, "There's nothing to forgive."

Eve began to cry as she leaned over and hugged me. She took out a tissue and said, "I'm sorry. I'm a mess."

I took her hand and smiled. "We're all a mess, aren't we?"

"You seem to have turned out okay. Mary said you even went to college."

"I did, but I didn't do it on my own. Aunt Edith was a big help. I know it's hard to believe, but we both found peace and strength in Jesus."

At the mention of Jesus, Eve leaned back in her chair.

"Mary said you went to church. Edith too. I'm glad for you. For both of you. As for me I'm still…trying to figure where I fit in. You know?"

I did know. I sensed her reticence and changed the subject. I told her all about my daughter and my job. Eve talked about her life with Arthur and how things had changed.

When we got back to the room, Eve said, "I don't think I can go back in there. I'm sorry, but it's all just too much."

"I understand. Eve, please don't be a stranger. Carli would love to meet you. Imagine a daughter of mine studying to become a doctor."

Eve smiled and said, "If she's anything like her mother she'll be great at whatever she does."

We said our goodbyes, and I took my place at my fading mother's bedside. Sitting there I was brought back to our last meeting. I closed my eyes and saw myself as I stood on the other side of the door and heard the lock click—the door frame hard and firm just like the woman on the other side.

An hour after Eve left, my mother, who up until this point hadn't spoken or given any sign she was really in there, began to rouse. Her eyes were still closed, but she raised her right hand and began to point at something. I pulled my chair up closer and leaned in.

"Mom? Mom?"

No answer. She continued to point with both her hands now. Feeling led to ask, I said, "Mom, what do you see?"

Words, as if coming from another realm, began to form on her cracked lips. "There…want to go…there."

"Go where, Mom?"

"Go to where all those people are, up on hill. The hill—green, so green."

I knew she was seeing a world beyond this one. Almost afraid to ask but sensing my prayers for God to meet her where she was were being answered I said, "Do you want to go to be with them? Be with…Jesus?"

"He's…there…can I go?"

The world was splitting apart, heaven reaching down into her hospital room. *I need to make this simple*. "All you have to do is ask."

She nodded ever so slightly. Her hands stopped moving and her tense expression began to relax.

"Mom, can you hear me?"

Silence. I sat back in my chair stunned at what had just happened. I closed my eyes and cried my thanks to God.

The air grew heavy. The sounds of the machines faded as His presence filled me, filled the room with a tangible peace. My mother, whose life had been a struggle from the start, who had never expected to receive absolution, was now free.

She passed an hour later into what I was certain were the waiting arms of Jesus.

2001

We were all gathered in the waiting room praying for good news from Harriet's daughter, Esther Ruth. Her pregnancy had been difficult and now the baby was a month early. Esther's husband, Will, was at her side, another difficulty Harriet, by her own admission, had not handled well. Theirs had been a quiet ceremony seeing she was already five months pregnant, but now a new life was coming—a life we were all there to celebrate.

It was hard to believe just three days ago the world exploded as planes tore into towers, tore into humanity. We all watched in horror as smoke and flames engulfed more than steel and glass.

How could anyone survive this? How can we survive this?

"It's a boy!" A gowned Will stood beaming. I turned to see handshakes and smiles all around. Minerva looked at me. She hugged her daughter and came over.

"I know."

I put on a weak smile. "Know what?"

"What you're thinking."

She always did.

"Is it…wrong to be celebrating anything now?"

Minerva nodded. "True enough, but we should never feel guilty giving thanks for a blessing even if it's in the midst of a terrible storm."

As one life entered this world thousands more had left it wanting.

In an instant, all my problems no longer mattered.

2019

Joe opened the door and peeked out. "Can I get you a blanket?"

"No, I'm fine, really. You've bundled me up already. Besides, the breeze feels good on my face." He came over and placed a gentle kiss on my cheek.

"Why don't you go and check on Mrs. Griffin. Her grandson stopped by yesterday and said she wasn't doing well."

"I hate to leave you alone, but even I know your favorite thing is to be alone on this porch."

He knew me so well.

He checked to see if he had his phone. "I won't be long. Do you have your…"

I patted my lap. "My phone is right here. Now go and let me think and rock to my heart's content."

He knelt down in front of me and placed his hands on mine. "How will I ever…"

"We both know how you will ever."

His tender hug, strong and reassuring, reminded me that one day soon I would be embraced by the One who would welcome me home.

Joe kissed me again and pulled the fleece cap down over my bald head. When he got to the bottom of the steps, he turned and said, "I love you, Alice. More than the days we count here; more than the ones we'll count there."

It was a silly thing we'd say, but we both believed in the promise of eternity. As he rounded the cabin, I closed my eyes and took as deep a breath as I was able. This man I married almost eleven years ago had softened me, taught me to lean into God's loving embrace. When we learned the cancer had returned with a vengeance stealing time and challenging hope, we fell into each other's arms and wept. The grief was a complicated sorrow, this transition, to be separated for a time but reunited in glory.

My thoughts were interrupted by the sound of children laughing. More and more have built homes here, raising their families and creating memories. A sadness began to well up.

There was so much more to do.

A still voice reminded me of how the deserts of my life had been turned into streams and my broken places restored. I smiled at the gentle reminder.

I had been blessed these past years. I'd watched my daughter achieve her dream and become the doctor we all knew she could be. And now her daughter, Alice Rosa, was following in her footsteps. At least that was the current plan. I worried over my granddaughter's tendency toward restlessness. I often prayed about what Edith called the legacy of thirst the women in our family carried, that it wouldn't lead her to search for fulfillment from a world ill-equipped to satisfy the cravings of the spirit.

I ran my hands back and forth over the smooth armrests. It was just last year when Carli and I sat on this very porch the day after my doctor visit. When I handed my daughter the deed to the cabin, she resisted but eventually took it and held the paper to her heart. It was too final of an act she said. After that, few words were spoken, were needed.

I was at peace.

As I looked around at new life springing forth, a small bird landed on the railing and just stared at me.

I was worth more than the sparrows.

The breeze intensified, and I pulled my comforter closer. I remembered something my aunt shared with me, words shared with her during a time of doubt and anger, words given to a mother she barely knew—to never forget how to listen to the wind, to breathe in the scents of God’s design, to see what He has done around you, and to always keep your eyes fixed on Jesus and on the wonder of what lies ahead.

I wondered what lay ahead as I tried to listen and breathe in what was around me. Had I left the details of the path to God? I pray I had.

Carlotta

October 2019

It was the perfect fall day. A strong breeze stirred up the water, made leaves fall like rain. They had all come—those who loved my mother and those who weren't certain how they felt. But today it didn't matter; nothing mattered except to say good-bye.

One by one they came through the woods. Children ran ahead, kicked pine cones away and brushed aside branches for those who carefully made their way with canes. My aunts, Genevieve and Mary, walked arm in arm to the water's edge. Dear Minerva braved the uneven path and pushed her sister, Esther, in a wheelchair.

Amends had been made over the years, relationships mended, forgiveness extended, tears accepted. My husband, Mateo, was the last to come down the path with our daughter, Alice Rosa.

I was here with my mother's ashes, finally ready to release her to the water. Holding the urn in one hand and a copy of her first published book of poems, *A Woman at the Well*, in the other I stood in the middle of a life redeemed by grace.

I walked over to the old pier by her beloved cabin and waited for everyone to settle. "There are benches and chairs for those who'd like to sit…"

Mary laughed and said, "Or need to sit, young lady."

"Thank you all for coming today. You've all meant so much to my mother and to me. At times the years have been hard, but through it all, God has sustained us by His gracious love."

"Amen to that," said Minerva.

Most agreed by head nods and *amens.* Children laughed behind me as they tossed stones and dipped their toes. I turned and smiled at their joy. "My mother loved this place, loved standing at the edge with her toes in the water. Said it was the only time she was able to touch two worlds at once—the firmness of land and the movement of water." I tightened my grasp on her book and felt like I was holding her hand.

"A few years ago, she shared with me she had been writing about the disparity of these images most of her life and never realized it." I was abruptly brought back to that poignant conversation when I sat next to her and watched the harsh treatment meant to prolong her life pump poison into her arm.

Unnerved by the force of the memory, I managed to continue. "But the image she said resonated the most with her was that of a well. 'You cannot hold water without a boundary stone' she would say…" I tried to laugh my way through the grief but failed miserably.

Seeing my pain, Alice's husband, Joe, came and placed his arm around me. "I remember my wife telling me she felt pulled to the story of the woman at the well, felt drawn to it like being pulled along by God's strong current to drink deep and long."

"That's right, Joe," agreed Esther. She sat upright in her wheelchair and pointed to the women gathered around. "Sisters, we are all women at the well of His living water who need to drink deeply."

We smiled at her wisdom.

Looking over at her granddaughter, Esther wagged her finger and said, "And don't you forget it, young lady."

Respectful laughter eased the tension. Joe gave me a gentle hug and went over to my daughter who had been desperately trying to hold it together.

"It's only fitting I begin by reading her favorite poem. She once told me this one even more than the others spoke of how she went from being what she called "thin-souled" to being filled to overflowing with peace and purpose."

I carefully opened the book and turned to the last page. As I spoke the words, I heard her voice:

My whole life searches for a word, runs for meaning. Thin-souled, dreaming shatters images like glass. I am lost.

I am there only out of habit. I hide beneath the mud of innuendo and suffocate my desire without notice.

I watch as Your prophet eyes follow my every move and look through me and see the demand of my thirst, a satisfaction that is beyond the power of water...but You already knew that.

Bone-dried and soul-scorched, the water I drink becomes the breath that pours into the space between our worlds.

The words You speak pierce and fracture the silent crimes that have labeled me fallen...

The passionate sacrifice of Your silence wraps around my stated indifference like a mantle and offers me life.

Baptized in a current of love, I am swept away...

My voice broke with the knowledge that I too had been carried away and restored. I looked at the understanding faces around me. My daughter, who had been standing behind her father, stepped out. She came to me and took my hand. "You can do this."

Could I?

Turning toward the lake and with my loudest voice I continued.

"Splintered soul, retrace your steps, return your heart..."

As my words—her words—echoed back, I closed my eyes and breathed in the fresh scent of nature.

My heart pounded as I closed the book and felt the breeze kiss my cheek. I bent down, set the urn next to me and almost nonchalantly touched the smooth tops of the nails that had risen above the pier's rough wood.

Life.

The only sound was the gentle sieve of her life between my fingers.

When I was done, I stood and tearfully faced my family. Opening to the end of her book, I read the last words of the poem as a testament, as an invitation—

"*Step out. The smoke is clearing.*"

Book Club
Discussion Questions

Prologue

Iris: 1800-1889. Even before we begin to discuss the other characters in the first section, let's talk about Iris. Her father has arranged for her to marry Walter, a man she barely knows.

What can you ascertain about Iris after reading, "obedience was more important than affection" and "another hasty decision made without my consent"?

We are told her husband has moved them to escape the "disease and sinful squalor" of the cities only to find themselves surrounded by "unrest and fear."

Discuss what you know about the time period and the possible causes.

Northern and Central New York becomes the setting for the stories that follow.

Not much is known about Iris except that she takes delight in the ordinary and often times difficult tasks related to her situation and the time in which she lives. Iris believes God will answer her prayer for her daughters and their daughters.

Why do you think she focuses on her daughters and not her male children? What struggles might be specific to a woman then and now?

A Necessary Melting

In this first part, the narrative jumps from Iris to her great-granddaughter, Merriam.

Merriam: 1878-1915.

Why do you think she was disappointed with her first daughter's "apparent contentment"?

Merriam suffered the unimaginable loss of three of her children, four if you count Mary Rose who ran away to marry an undesirable man.

Discuss Merriam's reticence to share her "youthful stories of imagined adventures" with her daughter.

How do you think the times affected a woman's willingness to share the intimate parts of her heart? How might a woman's willingness to open her heart to others still be affected today?

Mary Rose: 1895-1928. Mary Rose's narrative begins with a deep knowledge of the fragility of life. She learned early to "hold [her] tears like [her] mother did."

After the death of her brother, David, how might her life have been better if it was permissible to talk about your feelings?

We are introduced to her father's sister, Elizabeth, in this section and her "steps of prayer." Being the teacher that she was, she used what was around her to enlighten Mary Rose's mind.

Discuss her interaction with Mary on their walk to the lake.

Mary runs away with a man who her family believed to be unsuitable.

Discuss Mary's marriage and subsequent life with Edward. How did you feel when she allowed him back into her life?

Mary found peace when she went to the abandoned cabin in the woods.

Do you have a special place where you feel at peace?

At the end of her life as she lays on her deathbed, Mary Rose is reminded of the incident at the well where David died. But she doesn't leave this world without hope. She has come to a well where there is life and been satisfied with God's living water.

Because the narrative jumps from Iris to Merriam almost nothing is revealed about the life of Abigail, Iris' daughter, except when Iris tells us her daughter's reaction to her humming. We are also given a small glimpse into Charlotte's life when Merriam tells us her "mother's faith kept her intact but unable to push against her husband's edicts" and that "the severity of a woman's lot" was passed down to her mother and her.

Discuss how the legacy of those brief revelations might have impacted the next generation.

A Hard Resolve

In this next part, we are introduced to two of Mary Rose's daughters, Edith and Helen.

> Edith: 1923-1987. Edith's first memory is of her mother giving birth to her sister and wondering over the death of her brother. We learn early that she "was free to love the deep color" of the midwife's skin, a woman named Flora whose gentleness and understanding would influence Edith in the years to come.
>
> *What do think about her fear that, if she gave up her will, she would also "go directly to Jesus"? How important is it to explain death to children in a way that is neither frightening nor evasive?*
>
> As Edith matured, her understanding of the world changed. Even though she finally understood why Elijah was excluded, her love for him could not be contained.
>
> *Discuss Edith's leaving and living with Flora's cousin, Mabel, and her family. How do you feel about her leaving her child behind?*
>
> Mabel spoke about how her grandparents were evicted from their homes so "rich white folks could have more room to picnic."
>
> *Are you familiar with Seneca Village? There are many websites to research this sad chapter in our history.*

This section carries Edith into 1943 where we find her living with her great-aunt, Elizabeth. After she dies, Edith takes a position at a hotel where she meets Michael Denison, a man she eventually works for and falls in love with. He, like Edith, is carrying secrets that the world would not understand or accept. This relationship softens Edith for a time, but she once again pulls inward and hardens her heart when he dies.

Helen: 1928-1988. The distance between these sisters begins with Helen's words—"I never said I knew."

What must the weight have been like for this young girl to know her father and sister have lied to her?

This is also where the seeds of guilt Helen carried with her began to grow—the question about her part in the death of her mother and brother.

How does the burden of guilt shadow and shape our lives?

Helen's husband, Frank, is a simple yet complex character. He is a gentle soul who has been physically and emotionally wounded in the war.

How might this have added to Helen's downward spiral?

With the birth of her children, Helen pulls further away.

This distance and inadequacy she experiences as a mother only add to her insecurities. As the cabin becomes a blessing to Frank, Helen resists the pull to accept it. In her mind, the cabin and her absent sister cannot be separated. Helen begins to have a series of affairs resulting in the birth of Alice.

Is it possible that somewhere in Helen's mind she would have preferred her husband deny this child and show appropriate indignation instead of a quiet acceptance of something they both knew was a lie?

Waiting, a Pot Boiling

In part three, we are introduced to Helen's three daughters.

Genevieve/Eve: 1949-. Eve begins with, "Was there any story worth my time to tell?" She is a woman born in the middle of her sisters but lost without her twin brother, Frankie, who was killed in a car accident in 1961. She tells us about her family who she calls a "disastrous swirl of dysfunction," reporting more than relating, something that describes the way she lives her life.

How do the dynamics in our families affect the way we see ourselves? See the world?

Mary Agnes: 1947-. As the oldest daughter, Mary has difficulty seeing herself as an individual. Her flirt with religion left her wanting as did her marriage to Richard. This brief introduction into Mary's life helps us begin to understand and appreciate her struggles. She tells the reader her "life had become narrow by years of self-doubt."

Can you relate to Mary's inner struggle with self-doubt? How does this lack of confidence impact perspective and a sense of worth?

Alice: 1952-2019. Alice is a complex character, as much a child of the times as a child of a broken mother. She tells us she "was born at odds with myself" who was "accepted but kept at a distance by unspoken words and strained looks."

Have you ever experienced feeling at odds with yourself? Why?

Her life has been affected by her mother's poor choices, her life with Edith and the accident that set them all on a collision course with disaster. Coming of age in the turbulent Sixties, Alice took the injustices surrounding her personally. Because she believed herself to be helpless, her journal became her sounding board and confidant. Her flirt with the illegal and her subsequent marriage to Donato ill-prepared her for motherhood—history repeating itself.

Alice mentions a gift Mr. Jenkins gave her, a book of poems by another Alice. The book referred to is Alice Walker's book of poems, *Once.*

Alice says she never understood the cost of speaking out against the prejudice that eventually caused the book shop to close.

Discuss how speaking out for what you believe has a cost.

A Disjointed Narrative

The story continues with Alice moving in with her aunt after her husband, Donato, dies from an overdose. Edith is at first reticent to open her life up to her niece but understands enough to put aside her fears.

When she is older, Alice's daughter, Carlotta or Carli as she is called, asks about her father, something Alice never did. Hesitant to open an unknown door, she attempts to contact Carli's Uncle Carlos who she hasn't seen for a very long time.

This part is also where we are introduced to Minerva and her family. Edith has finally opened up about her former life, giving Alice an understanding of her past behavior. Alice is surprised over Minerva's acceptance of her daughter Harriet's unplanned pregnancy, especially after learning what happened to her aunt.

Discuss the similarities and differences in Edith's and Harriet's experiences.

The story strengthens with the revelation that Minerva's sister is Edith's daughter. Minerva shares pictures and stories with Alice, giving us a look into how Esther grew up.

News of Carlos' death impacts Carli and prompts Alice to finally go to church with Minerva.

How does tragedy and difficulty prompt us to seek a deeper meaning in life?

Alice is introduced to Joe who is speaking at church about "the purpose for the pain we carry."

After reading this sermon, do you agree/disagree with his reasoning? Why or why not?

Alice's narrative is interrupted by Mary Agnes who has acted on Oliver's invitation to go to Australia. The experience leaves her wanting, feeling like she "was caught in a rocker, baptized in a torrent of water seeking gold, being tossed by dirt and looking for anything of value."

Have there been experiences or events in your life that have made you feel this way?

Edith discovers she is very ill and decides to go to church with Alice. It is there she learns about intimacy with God and eternal hope, something she has secretly craved her whole life.

Have you ever felt the pull to get closer with God?

Felt Like a Sign

Part Five begins with Mary returning to the cabin because "she had the deep need to go back to where she lost herself, back to where they all lost everything." Up until this point, we are told very little about the accident. The experience unravels her, pulls her back into a past she has wanted to forget. She is shocked to see Alice, who she hasn't seen in twenty years, by a cabin that has been restored. They reconnect and, in like fashion, are restored to each other.

Mary calls her sister, Eve, asking she accompany her to see Edith. Eve doesn't want to go. She has borne the brunt of not only Edith's cold remarks but her mother's for too long. After Frankie dies, her mother has cruelly blamed her for his death. This is also the first time we get a glimpse into Eve's life with her husband, Arthur. Distance and disappointment have surrounded them, leading Eve to walk out. In the end, she resists the pull to run away and "steps back into the smallness of the elevator."

How do you feel about her decision not to leave?

Edith's life is coming to a close, and she's waiting for someone to come. Her daughter, Esther, is there to not only say goodbye but to say thank you. She also meets Grace, Esther's newly adopted baby. Edith dies at peace with her past. We are not told if Mary and Eve ever come to say goodbye.

Do you think they both showed up? Based on what you know about Mary and Eve, how do you feel it went?

At the close of this section, we find Helen still in a sad state. Alice attempts to connect but is met with resistance and antagonism.

Swept Away:

This last section begins about five years after Alice's visit when Helen's excess leads to a tragic car accident on Christmas Eve. The calls go out as each sister responds to the news differently. Mary, who we find has been volunteering at a soup kitchen, has softened over the years, looking beyond herself to discover her worth in helping others. She calls Eve who is hesitant to open herself back up to a mother who she has blamed for her shortcomings.

Discuss how blame, forged in the Garden of Eden when Adam blamed Eve for his weakness, can impact a life.

The news unsteadies Eve enough into vividly remembering the accident. We are brought back to 1961 and finally understand the depth of her pain.

Alice is there when Helen has an encounter with God, giving her a blessed assurance that her mother is finally at peace.

Have you ever had an experience like Alice with someone who is passing?

There is brief mention in this section about the tragedy that occurred on 9/11. This brevity is not meant to diminish but to acknowledge the heartbreak and pain this terroristic act caused "as one life entered this world, thousands more had left it wanting."

Discuss your memories of this time.

The current of our story begins to slow in the spring of 2019 as Alice, who is dying of cancer, is back at her cabin. She reminisces about her life and is reminded "of how the deserts of [her] life had been turned into streams and [her] broken places had been restored." She remembers the words Edith shared with her, "words shared with her during a time of doubt and anger, words spoken to a mother she barely knew."

Discuss their meaning and truth.

The last voice we hear is that of Alice's daughter, Carlotta. Family and friends have gathered at the lake to say goodbye and spread Alice's ashes. She is finally able to share her words with others through her published book of poems.

Have you ever tried to write about the important times in your life? Try doing that now, whether in a poem or just a few words.

What do you think the last words, "Step out. The smoke is clearing" might mean for you?

Final Thoughts

Consider the choices the author makes: only a few of the characters have last names and although we are told in the prologue that Iris and her husband have moved to Northern New York, there is only one city referred to by name (Albany). It can be assumed the story is set in the northeast, most likely New York State, but it is only alluded to.

Do you feel the absence of these details added to or detracted from the story the women were telling?

Discuss the repeating themes in the story: the time of year (fall), the cabin and lake, and the well.

Discuss the characters. Were there any you identified with? Why? Which one evoked the strongest reaction?

Discuss the story as a whole. Did you have a favorite part? Read this section aloud to the group.

Were there any similarities between you and your family's story and the one you just finished reading?

Now that you know Alice's story, reread the poem "The Current of Water" that appears at the beginning of the book.

What questions about your life, your choices, have come to the surface after reading the story?

Detailed Character Timeline

1790: Walter born; married Iris when he was twenty-five

1800: Iris born: married Walter when she was fifteen

1815: Abigail born: Iris's daughter

1838: Abigail marries Luther (she's 23)

1839: Charlotte born: Abigail's daughter

1857: Elizabeth born

1868: Flora born: midwife

1874: Cabin at the lake built; Elizabeth's fiancé dies

1875: Charles born: marries Merriam

1878: Merriam born: Charlotte's daughter

1889: Edward born: marries Mary Rose

1893: Mika Denisov (Michael Denison) born: Edith's boss/friend; he is thirty when Edith is born

1894: Jonathan born: marries Mary Rose after Edward dies

1895: Merriam marries Charles; grandfather to Edith and Helen

1895: Mary Rose born: Merriam's daughter

1897: James born—dies: Merriam's son

1889: Iris dies (89)

1890: Charlotte dies (71)

1898: Emma born-dies: Merriam's daughter

1900: Abigail dies (85)

1900: David born: Merriam's son

1903: David dies (3)

1904: Mabel born: Flora's cousin

1910: Charlotte dies (71)

1914: Mary Rose marries Edward

1914: William born: Jonathan's younger step-brother

1915: Andrew born: Merriam's last child

1915: Walter born—dies: Mary Rose's child

1915: Merriam dies (37)

1916: Lillian born—dies: Mary Rose's child

1921: Mildred born: Mary Rose's child

1921: Mary Rose told to leave and moves in with her father

1921: Elijah born: love interest of Edith; Flora's grandson

1922: Edward killed (33)

1923: Mary Rose marries Jonathan

1923: Edith born: Mary Rose and Jonathan's first child

1927: Frank born: Helen's future husband

1928: Mary Rose dies in childbirth (33)

1928: Andrew born

1928: Helen born: Mary Rose and Jonathan's second child

1939: Millie and William marry

1940: Edith moves in with Mabel and her husband, John; Mabel's children: Simon: born 1925, Harriet: born 1930; Ruth: born 1933; Anne: born 1935, Minerva: born 1943

1940: Esther born: Edith's child

1941: Edith moves in with her great-aunt, Elizabeth

1942: Flora dies (74)

1943: Minerva born: younger step-sister of Esther

1943: Elizabeth dies (86)

1944: Jonathan marries Margaret

1945: Margaret dies (50)

1946: Helen marries Frank

1946: Edith moves in with Michael (Mika)

1947: Mary Agnes born: Helen and Frank's first child

1948: Millie dies in childbirth (23)

1949: Frankie and Genevieve/Eve born: Helen and Frank's children

1951: Jonathan dies (57)

1952: Alice born: illegitimate daughter of Helen

1955: Frank Sr. dies (33)

1956: Mika dies (63); leaves Edith money to buy a small house

1958: Helen and her children move in with Edith

1958: Esther, Edith's daughter, marries; husband's name is Frederick

1960: Esther has son, James

1961 Frankie Jr. dies in car accident (12)

1962: Helen sells deed to cabin to Edith

1962: Helen and her three children move out of Edith's and move in with her boyfriend

1963: Harriet born: Minerva's daughter

1964: Mary Agnes leaves for college

1967: Eve marries Arthur

1970: Mary Agnes marries Richard

1971: Alice gets married right out of high school to Donato

1972: Edith born, Esther's youngest daughter

1972: Carlotta born: Alice and Donato's daughter

1972: Donato dies (23)

1972: Alice moves in with Edith

1973: Esther and her husband adopt three siblings (two girls and a boy)

1974: Rickie born: Mary and Richard's son

1976: Mary Agnes divorces Richard

1979: Mabel dies (73)

1980: Esther Ruth born; Harriet's daughter

1982: Alice becomes a Christian

1984: Mary goes to Australia

1986: Edith becomes a Christian

1987: Edith dies (64)

1989: William dies (75)

1992: Helen dies in a car accident (64)

1994: William dies (80)

1998: Carlotta marries Mateo

1998: Alice marries Joe Clarke (she's 47)

1999: Alice Rosa born: Carlotta and Mateo's daughter

2001: Esther Ruth gets married; already five months pregnant; husband's name is Will; has a son

2019: Alice dies (67)

Made in the USA
Middletown, DE
10 March 2023

26406127R00142